RP

THE TEXANS

**Center Point
Large Print**

**This Large Print Book carries the
Seal of Approval of N.A.V.H.**

THE TEXANS

D. B. NEWTON

CENTER POINT PUBLISHING
THORNDIKE, MAINE

This Center Point Large Print edition
is published in the year 2004 by arrangement with
Golden West Literary Agency.

The text of this Large Print edition is unabridged. In other
aspects, this book may vary from the original edition. Printed in
Thailand. Set in 16-point Times New Roman type by
Bill Coskrey and Gary Socquet.

ISBN 1-58547-416-9

Cataloging-in-Publication data is available from the Library of Congress.

THE TEXANS

CHAPTER I

Ben Murdock came in off the herd ground with a strong wind blowing up behind him, running in waves through the tough prairie grass and pressing him forward like a hand against his back. His pony didn't like the wind or the constant lightning, and by now every rumbling of thunder had it ready to jump out of its skin. Murdock needed a firm hand to steady the animal. But at least, with perhaps two hours to daybreak, the rain was still holding off.

At the trail camp, wind snapped the canvas of the wagons with reports like gunshots, and might have done real damage if the wheels of both rigs hadn't, as usual, been solidly staked down. The wind stirred up some last embers of the cook's fire and sent them spiraling in glowing streaks toward the cloud ceiling. On the picket line the horses were moving about restlessly. Most of the men were out of their bedrolls but a few still managed to sleep, too exhausted after sixteen hours in the saddle to be disturbed by the threat of a storm about to break on top of them. As Murdock reined in, the ones who had been uncertainly standing around hurried up. He answered questions with scant patience.

"They're holding so far, but they don't like this any; it wouldn't take nothing at all for us to lose them." He indicated the sleeping figures. "Get the others up—we're going to need everybody! Move!"

They split, running to get their horses off the picket line and to strap on saddles that, in some cases, had barely had time to cool after a stint at night guard. One or two took it on themselves to boot the sleeping men awake and bring them grumbling out of their blankets. Murdock considered switching to a fresh mount, but decided not to use the time. The bay he rode was a sturdy animal, and though it had been ridden for a lot of hours he knew he could still count on it unless this thing turned into a run. But that was just what he was figuring to prevent, rather than see nearly five thousand head of beef scattered to hell and gone across empty Kansas prairie.

Over by the bedroll wagon, the tarp Wilson Stiles customarily rigged for a shelter—judging it to be his special due, as one of the owners of the big Pool herd—had been ripped free of its anchorage to one of the wheels. The wind was tearing at it, whipping the heavy material about, and a flicker of lightning showed Stiles on his feet and struggling to get the canvas under control again. When Murdock reined over to him he had to shout to make himself heard.

"Having a little trouble?"

The shuttering play of lightning revealed both men: Stiles, well built and rangy and bareheaded, the thick strands of yellow hair blowing about his face; Murdock, considerably younger than the other's thirty-five years—a stocky figure in the saddle, broad hatbrim pulled well down against the weather and shadowing the stubborn shape of the trail boss's jaw and broad cheekbones. Animosity that had been building, even before this drive left the plains of distant Texas, lay open between them as Ben Murdock indicated the blowing tarp and said, "Afraid you'll have to leave it for now. I've got to have every man available out there on the herd."

The tarp was forgotten. Stiles left it tearing wildly at its lashings as he straightened and came about. He said in a cold voice, "Are you giving me an order?"

"Much as I know it gravels you," Murdock answered, "I've got the job of delivering this herd— and that includes giving orders. Right now there's need for every man that can sit a horse, with no exceptions. So get saddled!"

He reined away, not waiting for a reply, pressured by his responsibilities at the herd ground where this night hung in the balance.

Already the men he had called up were mounting and spurring off in that direction. At the messwagon he saw the cook, a man no one ever called anything but George. Like most such, he had been a puncher, until old age and the crippling effects of too many spills from the saddle grounded him to his present job. George was lath-lean and balding. He stood clutching a timber of the wagon as though to keep from being plucked away. As Ben Murdock rode past he called out against the tumult of the wind, "What was all that with Stiles? Does his lordship object to doing a little work, like some ordinary cowhand?"

"He objects to me telling him he has to."

The old cook wagged a bony head. "If *I* owned part of this herd, seems I'd want to lend a hand and keep it from scattering from hell to breakfast. But I guess some gents are more concerned with the principle of things than with common sense."

"I think it bothers his pride."

"Yeah. . . . Pride's a nice thing to have, for the guy who can afford it! Look," the old man added as the trail boss began to move away, "I ain't good for a lot, but if you want me I can maybe sit a saddle. . . ."

"No, George," Murdock told him. "Best way you can help is to have plenty of hot coffee ready for the boys—that is, if you can manage to get a fire going in this!"

He left the wagons and spurred off toward the dark mass of the herd.

The play of lightning was almost constant now; his eyes ached from it. The air held a faint tang of ozone, and thunder rolled steadily across the low-riding roof of clouds. Yet the rain still held off, though now he could feel an occasional needle-sharp stab of it riding the wind that pummeled him. That wind, off sun-scorched miles, was still warm; the spears of moisture that struck his face were ice-cold.

He would very soon be needing his slicker from behind the saddle. For the time being he left it where it was.

A steady, uneasy lowing rose from the herd now. Made restless by the uneasy night and by their own dumb fears, more cattle than before seemed to be on their feet, heads lifted to test the wet wind, but a lot were still down. That could change, of course, in an instant. A bolt of lightning slamming into the earth, a ball of St. Elmo's fire rolling across their horns, a shattering peal of thunder just overhead—at no more than this they could be off and running before you knew it.

The only thing more unpredictable than a longhorn steer was a bunch of them; and this was a very large bunch indeed, nearly five thousand head—almost twice the size of any other Kansas-bound trail outfit Ben Murdock had heard of in this August of 1872. It was a mixed herd, in several brands, since none of the small-scale Texas stockmen making up the Pool had more than a few hundred head they could throw in. Originally the plan had been to divide the drive in two, one section under the command of Tom Lindsay, who had been a key figure in organizing the Pool; Murdock, a young man with experience and a growing reputation, had been hired for the second. An unlucky accident in the breaking corral had put Lindsay out of action at the last minute, unable to join the drive. No other competent trail driver being available at a wage the Pool could afford, Ben Murdock had reluctantly agreed to assume the entire job himself.

So far he had managed to bring the whole unwieldy mass of cattle, and a mixed crew of riders from a dozen different brands, to within a few days of the goal at Ellsworth market. But before tonight was over, he had a hunch he was going to earn his pay.

A rider came quartering toward him, singing out his name. By fitful lightning flare Murdock recognized Vern Hoyt, one of the four hands supplied by Tom Lindsay of the Box L. Hoyt was a generally unsmiling man, nearing forty-five—a truly seasoned age for a cowpuncher. He had proved himself the most reliable member of the crew and had quickly settled into the post of second-in-command, though he couldn't be persuaded to take over a section of the herd himself. He drew up alongside Murdock now, their mounts standing head-to-tail, manes and tails tossing in the wind. He said, "Looks like it's touch and go. They're getting mean. Can you hear the difference?"

Murdock could. The constant mutter of the herd had grown louder, taking on a note almost of desperation. "I've called up the rest of the boys. Don't know what the chances are, but we can at least try to stop a run before it begins. You take this edge of the herd; I'll swing north and meet you at the far side."

"Right." About to pull away, Vern Hoyt lingered to add, "I just seen something that looked like that skewbald gelding of Stiles's. Don't tell me you actually put him to work."

"I sort of persuaded him."

The segundo said dryly, "That would have been interesting to see. I can tell you, some of the boys have been laying bets as to when the blowup was coming."

"There wasn't any blowup," Murdock said gruffly. "There isn't going to be. *I'm* sure not looking for one."

"But Stiles is! Everybody in the outfit knows he's got it in for you. He ain't satisfied that he has the Pool's authority to dispose of this herd for them at Ellsworth—he wanted *your* job for that foreman of his. He blames you for doing him out of it."

"Tate Corman would never have the savvy to manage a trail outfit like this one."

"You don't have to tell me! Corman's a loudmouth

and a bully. He'd have had the crew in a full-scale rebellion before they got much more than half this far. . . ."

The trail boss had no comment. The two split, riding their separate ways.

Ben Murdock, circling north of the dark and sullen mass of cattle, was very quickly joined by some of the crew he had ordered out to help the night guard. With a few terse words of instruction he sent half to report to Vern Hoyt and took the rest, dropping them off, one at a time, at points about the edge of the herd. He was still handling this task when the rain suddenly let go. It came down with a smash.

Murdock was caught unprepared, his slicker still lashed behind the saddle. He turned and fumbled at the tie-strings, and was soaked to the skin before he could jerk them free. But even then he didn't put the garment on, for as he started to shake it out a sizzling streak of chain lightning fried the sky and thunder broke overhead, and through a glistening curtain of rain he saw sudden activity at the herd.

Scarcely thinking, he jerked the bay around, the trained cowpony spinning under him. The steer that flash of lightning had shown him was a big fellow with a wicked spread of horns, and it loosed a bellow of fear as it started to bolt in his direction. Murdock didn't give an inch. Instead he leaned and swung his slicker at the beast's head, a little surprised to find it dimly visible through the rain—a first glimmer of dawn, he realized, was beginning to leak into the tumbled cloud ceiling. The heavy slicker caught the steer before it could build momentum, and it veered wildly off at a different angle. But it did not get far. A second puncher had seen what was happening, and he cut in and quickly drove it back into the herd.

Ben Murdock, however, recognized the signals, and they told him these animals were only moments away from a stampede. He swore, and kicked with the spur. As he went past that other rider he shouted above the din of the storm: "Turn them!" And then he was riding directly against a mass of panicked cattle, with the rain beating in his face and the ground turning to slop underfoot, using the heavy, rubbery material of his slicker as a flail.

Whatever might be happening elsewhere on the bedground, every animal in this part of the herd seemed to be on its feet and ready to move. Under such circumstances it was perilous to work so close to the razorsharp horns that could gut a man or a horse in a single slashing movement. Murdock never even thought about it; he knew other men were taking the same risk, and that their chances of keeping the herd under control hung on their quickness and determination. Cursing, brandishing coats or blankets or coils of rope or whatever else was at hand, they charged the scared beasts and time and again sent them back when they tried to bolt. And their efforts were bringing results.

As the first faint light of dawn began to strengthen through the steady rain, it was clear they were actually keeping them bunched and totally confused; Murdock sensed that the entire herd, frustrated in its urge to scatter, was being forced instead to turn in on itself. Bellowing and protesting, it was moving now like a great wheel of flesh and hoof and horn, beginning to revolve ponderously on its own axis.

Once that started, any seasoned trailhand knew the worst was over. . . .

Vern Hoyt nursed the cup of scalding coffee George had handed him, and fought the trembling in his legs that told of a strenuous night, of fatigue and letdown after the gut effort made to save the herd. It had taken more than an hour to be certain the cattle were settled, and by then it was dawn and the storm had finally blown away. Now, with daylight, the last clouds had scattered and an August sun was already pouring its heat along the edge of the flat prairie to set a wet earth steaming.

It promised to be another scorcher.

Above the rim of his cup Hoyt watched the camp activity, very much like that of any other morning. Just as usual George was stumping around his wagon, cleaning up after breakfast, stowing gear in preparation for rolling out when Ben Murdock gave the command. Yonder, a couple of the hands were trying to shake the mud out of soaked and trampled blankets. On the bedground the herd was feeding peaceably enough under the watchful eyes of the morning shift. All the panic, the near-stampede that never happened, seemed completely forgotten. Meanwhile the nighthawk was jingling his big remuda toward the rope corral, where the day's first mounts would be cut out and saddled.

Hoyt flipped away the dregs of his coffee and walked

over to dump the tin cup into the wreck pan on the messwagon's lowered tailgate. As he did he saw a knot of men who stood talking together: Wilson Stiles, Sherm Watkins, and Jed Finch—three Pool members who had chosen to accompany their beef on the trail to market. In last night's emergency these men had risked their necks, the same as any of the crew, but now that that was over they stood once more apart and aloof, across a gulf that separated owner from thirty-a-month hand.

Jed Finch caught sight of Hoyt and at once jerked an arm at him, a summoning gesture that caused Hoyt's mouth to settle in an expression of dry distaste. Finch might be one of the bosses in this joint drive, but he wasn't much by any standards Vern Hoyt respected. A lantern-jawed fellow whose mean eyes seemed to crowd the bridge of his nose, Finch had earned his status as a full-fledged Pool member by contributing just 180 head of beef to this drive—beef that he'd gleaned (or so Vern Hoyt was ready to guess) by use of an easy loop and a ready running iron. He had also contributed himself, along with his brother Pike—a raw-boned, slightly younger version of himself—and a dull-eyed and nearly useless hand they called Gater. Being allowed to hang around with the other owners, just as though he were their equal, no doubt gave his ego a big lift.

It galled Vern Hoyt to answer his summons. He liked it no better when Finch told him, as if he were someone ordering a livery hostler to bring around his horse: "Go find Murdock."

16

Hoyt returned the man's stare and said, "Go find him yourself. Whatever he's busy with, he's not going to drop it and come running on your say-so."

The mean little eyes flared. Jed Finch started an angry retort but Sherm Watkins, always the peacemaker, said quickly, "That's all right. I'm afraid we're all short-tempered after last night." Hoyt accepted the comment with a shrug. He liked Watkins well enough—judged him, in fact, the best man in the Pool after his own boss, Tom Lindsay. There was dignity and patience in the lean face with the downswept, grizzled mustache. On the other hand, Watkins was not a young man anymore and the rigors of this drive had clearly put their mark on him. "We're wondering," he continued, "what Murdock has in mind about moving 'em out as usual, after last night."

"He hasn't told me," Vern Hoyt said. "But I imagine he'll be wanting to push on."

Wilson Stiles said harshly, "Damn it, he thinks he can drive men like they were horses!"

Hoyt gave him a quick glance, thinking, *Lucky for you, or right now you'd personally have about six hundred head of beef scattered clean across the face of Kansas!* He said tersely, "I'll see what I can find out."

As he left them, he was thinking that Ben Murdock surely must have known the trouble he was in for in attempting to serve too many masters—the dozen members of the Pool, all of them small ranchers more or less jealous and suspicious of one another. It didn't help any having three members of the Pool underfoot on the drive, criticizing and even countermanding his

17

orders if they felt like it; nor was it easy being stuck with a herd of such unwieldy size—a herd such as no one had ever before been called on to deliver—and a crew made up of riders loyal only to their particular brands.

Hoyt was reminded of an old saying about one rotten apple spoiling a barrelful. An outfit this size was bound to have a few, and most of those seemed to be men who rode for Wilson Stiles—like his segundo, Tate Corman, who'd thought he should be handed Murdock's job as trail boss. And here, crossing his path, was yet another one, Dab Pollard, who favored Hoyt with an idle stare as he tramped past on the way to the roping pen with a bridle slung across one shoulder, huge Mexican spur rowels chiming.

Dab Pollard was another Stiles puncher, a compactly built man with a too-easy smile that somehow never quite seemed to touch his cool and watchful eyes. It had turned out that he belonged to the breed of trail-camp cardsharps, and no one, by Hoyt's reckoning, rated lower than a man who would ring marked decks in what were supposed to be friendly games meant to ease the monotony of a long drive. By the time he was exposed the damage had already been done. Dab Pollard, with his victims mostly plucked, had simply sneered at them, smug in his own cleverness; and because they were afraid of him, or afraid of the crew he rode with, none of those Pollard had cheated seemed willing to risk making a challenge.

But bitterness remained, and in Vern Hoyt's opinion it was helping to tear this outfit apart. The Pool, he thought, should be grateful to Ben Murdock for holding things together as long as he had. Two months behind them now, with Ellsworth—and trail's end—all but in sight . . .

When he located the man he was looking for, Hoyt could sense at once that there was some new trouble. Murdock, his expression grave, was talking to the night-wrangler, a Mexican lad named Rafael who helped out with the remuda and drove the bedroll wagon for the cook. They were examining a horse the young fellow held by the reins, a strawberry roan under saddle. Vern Hoyt recognized it as one of those assigned to Wally McKay, a Box L rider. He noticed that the roan's left side was well plastered with drying mud, and one rein had been broken off short as if the animal had stepped on it.

Rafael was explaining, "I jus' now find him in the remuda, Señor Ben. I don' know when he's drift in. All that mud—he's look like something bad happen maybe."

Ben Murdock turned as Hoyt came up. "Vern, you know this animal?" Apparently he did himself, for without waiting for the other's nod he added bruskly, "You seen Wally McKay?"

"Not since last night," Hoyt said. "He was with me for a while, helping to get them cattle settled. After that I don't remember seeing him. You certain he ain't out pulling a shift?"

Murdock shook his head impatiently. "No. Oh, damn it!" He struck the heel of a fist against his forehead, a gesture filled with anger at himself. Hoyt spoke quickly, seeing the dark run of the man's thoughts: "Ben, don't blame yourself. You've got more than enough for one man to handle. You can't be responsible for everything!"

"I can, and I have to!" Murdock retorted harshly. "It's my job!"

"But there wasn't a stampede or anything. No reason at all to suppose—"

The trail boss cut him off. "Hurry! Get some of the boys. We've wasted too much time already."

It was the remaining three Box L punchers—friends of Wally McKay's, who had known him in Lindsay's bunkhouse before this drive began—who fell in to make the search. Murdock led them in a sweep of that section of the herd ground where McKay had last been seen. The newly risen sun was already sucking up streamers of mist from the soaked ground; by noon all signs of the rain would probably be gone and the prairie left baking again and powder-dry under merciless August heat. Vern Hoyt could feel the sweat already streaming. He said, "It don't seem possible he could have had an accident and us not be seeing any sign of it. Like his bronc taking a fall with him . . ."

"Far as that goes he could have been hung up in the stirrup and dragged," Murdock pointed out. "We'll look awhile."

The drying slop, marked by a confused jumble of many hoofprints, precluded looking for tracks. All they could do was move out from the herd in a widening circle, a slow process since they couldn't risk missing the one they were hunting. Flat as this country was, there were bush clumps and hollows where a man could lie without being noticed. With every minute that passed, chances of finding him alive would grow more remote.

And then a shout from one of the riders told that McKay had been found, face down in a swale some hundred and fifty yards from the herd where the roan must have dragged him. The swale had been turned into a puddle by the storm, and all these hours Wally McKay had been lying there half submerged. At first glance Hoyt thought the man was dead, but the one who had found him looked up to report, "He's breathing! But he's got a broke leg."

Ben Murdock stepped down to check the situation himself. "Fetch something from camp for splints and a bandage. And tell Rafael to bring the bedroll wagon."

The break was a bad one, near the hip. When Murdock carefully worked the hurt man's jeans down so they could see the damage, the sight of a grotesque bend in the leg where none should be was enough to make a man swallow a few times to keep his breakfast down. Ben Murdock said stolidly, "It's like we thought. The roan slipped and fell on him, and then dragged him when his boot hung up in the stirrup. Shock has knocked him out. We'll have to do something with that leg before we can move him."

The splints were brought, and a couple of dishtowels contributed by George, the camp cook. Murdock selected his materials, laid the splints into place, and tore the cloth into strips. Ordering Hoyt to hold the unconscious man steady, he seized the leg and gave it a steady pull. Hoyt thought he heard the broken ends of the thigh bone grind into place. McKay groaned and made a convulsive movement that almost tore him loose from the hands that held him, and then fell limp again. Minutes later, the strips of cloth wrapped about the splints, Murdock got to his feet and rubbed a palm across his sweating cheeks as he looked at the result of his crude frontier surgery. "What he needs is a doctor," he said gruffly. "But this is the best we can do."

The bedroll wagon came rattling up, and with great care the injured man was lifted inside. He was beginning to rouse, and somebody produced a half-filled bottle of whiskey. When they got some of it down him it set him coughing, and his body, after long hours of soaking in the chill ground water, shook violently. Ben Murdock palmed the cork home and set the bottle aside.

"Take it easy," he said as the hurt man tried to push himself up. "You got a leg broken." *And maybe worse than that,* Hoyt thought. "Can you remember what happened?"

He could, and he described the spill when his horse turned too suddenly in the slick and went down with him. "When he began dragging me, I thought I was a goner," McKay admitted hoarsely. "Till I managed to shake my boot free somehow. But I knew the leg was broke and I could only lie there and listen to the rest of you settling the herd."

Murdock said, "Why was that? You had a gun. Couldn't you have fired off a couple of shots?"

McKay dismissed that idea with all a cowhand's

22

single-minded dedication to the job that paid his thirty a month and beans. "And started 'em running, maybe? I did yell a few times, loud as I was able, but I guess no one heard me. No one, that is, except . . ."

"Except who?" the trail boss prompted.

"Maybe I imagined it—I was just about gone by that time, I reckon. But I thought I seen somebody ride up and stop there, maybe thirty feet from me. I was sure he noticed me. I tried to holler again but I dunno how much sound come out. And then I saw him turn and ride away again, and that's about the last I knew. I must have blanked out then."

"This rider," Ben Murdock said quietly, "who was it?"

The man shook his head. "I never saw him clear. Like I said, I'd think I just dreamed the whole thing . . . if it wasn't for the horse. . . ."

"And what about the horse?"

"Well . . ." Wally McKay answered reluctantly, "it sure looked to me like that skewbald gelding of Wilson Stiles's!"

What he saw in Murdock's face, as the trail boss heard that, gave Vern Hoyt a sudden chill.

CHAPTER II

Back at camp, things were nearly ready to start the day's work—horses roped and saddled, wagons ready to roll, punchers waiting for the order to mount. News of what had happened to Wally McKay spread rapidly; such an accident could have struck any member of the crew, and that was a thought that sobered them all. Ben Murdock let Hoyt answer the questions. He deliberately brushed them off and, stony-faced, went searching for Wilson Stiles.

He found him, together with the four members of his personal crew. The way they pretended not to notice Murdock as he came up told him a lot. It was only when he spoke Stiles's name that their heads turned. Stiles's expression was nearly unreadable, but Tate Corman, the hulking puncher who had expected to get Ben Murdock's job on this drive, wore a look of plain hostility that was matched by Dab Pollard, the marked deck artist.

Murdock confronted their boss. "We're bringing in a hurt man. He's got a smashed leg, no telling what else. His horse fell with him in the storm and left him lying out there."

Stiles, with pursed lips, appeared to consider this, but apparently found it of no personal concern. "Every man takes his chances," he said indifferently.

"That's true," Ben Murdock said coldly. "Still, I'd like to hear you explain how you could turn your back on a man when you heard him calling to you for help!"

"Who says——?" the other began, but something he saw in Murdock's face may have changed his mind, and the denial turned into a shrug. "Sure, I heard him. But a man able to yell that loud couldn't be too bad hurt, and we had a herd ready to start running at any minute."

"And when it didn't run? What about then, Stiles? With the cattle safe, and your own men all right, you never gave Wally McKay another thought—is that the way it was?" Unable to restrain himself, Murdock shook his head as he declared in a tone of anger and disgust, "You really are a sonofabitch, aren't you!"

He knew at once he had said too much. About to turn away, he caught a warning in the blond man's face. Clearly, this time Stiles had been stung past the point of reason. One hand dropped quickly toward his gunbelt; Murdock, having no weapon, had to move and it had to be fast. His right arm swept forward, and he felt a sudden aching impact as his knuckles struck the solid bone of the other man's jaw.

Someone loosed a shout of alarm as Wilson Stiles was knocked completely off his feet. He sprawled awkwardly in the mud, and his face went through a series of expressions—surprise, and shock, and then fury that sent the blood rushing into his cheeks. But the trail boss was right on top of him and spoke a quick warning: "Stiles, touch that gun and I'll kick your arm off! I mean it!"

Perhaps belatedly, Stiles realized he had tried to draw on an unarmed man. In any case, the gun stayed where it was. Murdock waited, watchful, as Wilson Stiles came to his hands and knees and from there to his feet. At that moment Sherm Watkins hurried up, exclaiming, "Here! Here! What is this?"

Ben Murdock shook his head. "Let him tell you if he wants."

"I'll tell you one thing!" Stiles said. The congestion of blood had drained from his face, leaving an unnatural pallor and a brightness in his stare, and the place where Murdock's knuckles had struck stood out darkly against his cheek. "Nobody uses his fists on me! This man and I have something that has to be settled!"

"Not as far as I'm concerned," Murdock answered shortly. "But if you want it I'm ready. Because you don't need to think I'm going to apologize!"

Watkins looked from one to the other in consternation. "I don't know what this is all about, but—my God! we've come five hundred miles, with Ellsworth less than a week to go. It's no time to fight among ourselves. We got a herd to deliver!"

"All right, go ahead," Wilson Stiles told him. "Deliver it." He had scooped up the hat he lost when he fell. He looked at the mud on his trouser leg, grimaced and gave it an angry swipe with the hatbrim. "But you'll do it without me," he added, dragging his hat on. "Because for once I've had enough. I'm getting out!" He turned away with a jerk of the head that summoned his men to follow, and strode to where the skewbald stood waiting under saddle.

He issued curt orders, and was turning to pull up the cinches when Sherm Watkins caught up with him, his

26

weathered features puckered with concern. "What are you talking about? Where do you think you're off to?"

The other gave him the briefest of glances. "Where would you think? Ellsworth, of course. Only, I travel alone—I prefer the company! Or do you *want* to see a showdown between this man and me, right here?"

As the older man gnawed at his lip in consternation, Vern Hoyt spat into the dust and said sourly, "Was it up to me, I'd let him go! Hell knows he's been spoiling for trouble, ever since Ben Murdock was hired to rod this drive!" As he spoke, one of the cowhands Stiles had sent off on an errand returned from the bedroll wagon with a roll of blankets and other personal possessions his boss would need on the trail. At a word from Stiles the man proceeded to tie the bundle in place behind the skewbald's cantle.

Sherm Watkins tried again. "I sure wish you wouldn't do it! I know you two haven't got along, but *this*—it can only mean the breakup of the Pool! After all our hard work . . ."

"Not at all," Wilson Stiles said crisply. "Only thing it means is that, traveling light, I'll be hitting Ellsworth a couple days before the rest of you. By time you come dragging in with the herd, I'll probably have a deal set up and all ready to close. I'm leaving Tate Corman behind; he can represent me."

"Do us a favor," Vern Hoyt suggested, "and take him with you."

That earned him a venomous glance from Corman. Stiles, his decision made, turned to his horse and swung astride. As he did, Dab Pollard came hurrying with a

27

sack of what looked to be trail rations he'd got from George. He handed it up and Stiles laid it across his lap. With the reins in his hand, he paused long enough for a last look at Ben Murdock. "We'll take up our differences another time!" he promised darkly.

Murdock answered, "That's up to you."

Sherm Watkins tried one last time. "No!" It was too late. Stiles spun his horse with a wrench of the reins and a kick of the spur. The animal leaped forward, iron shoes raising a gout of mud from the drying ground. The men of the trail crew, as though still bewildered by this turn of events, stood and watched as Wilson Stiles rode out of the camp—a spare and arrogant figure, easily erect in the saddle, glinting in the morning sun as its rays struck spur chain and saddle trappings and the brass that studded his cartridge belt. He rode steadily, not looking back, and the tawny plains rolling northward under the wide sky gradually absorbed the diminishing shapes of horse and rider.

Ben Murdock drew a breath. The thing was over. He looked at Watkins, and at the men who had been waiting beside their saddled mounts for word to start for the herd ground and get the drive moving. "All right," he said. "We're only losing time. Mount up— let's roll 'em."

Several moved automatically to obey, but almost at once the movement faltered. Glancing around, Ben Murdock discovered the reason: He saw Tate Corman standing exactly as before, arms akimbo, a defiant look on his broad face as he watched Murdock. The look was a challenge, and everyone there—not only the members of Corman's crew, his friends and followers such as Pollard and Jed Finch—realized the challenge must be met, or this drive was going to be stalled in its tracks. Murdock saw it clearly, and accepted it. In a sudden stillness, broken by the sweep of hot wind through the grass and the stomping of restless horses, he walked directly over to Corman.

"All right, Tate," he said. "It doesn't take a mind reader to know what you're thinking. You've been waiting for the chance to tell me where I could go; you probably figure this is it. Well, let me remind you of something," he went on, his voice like a whipcrack. "Your boss may have left you to take over for him, but Wilson Stiles still has six hundred head of beef in this drive. If anything happens to that beef because you didn't pull your weight, you're going to have to do some explaining—not to me, but to *him*. So I think you'd better quit this! Get your men on their horses and see that they get to work!"

Tate Corman glared, but as he saw that he had no choice, his mocking look turned angry and then almost petulant. He let the trail boss see all the hatred that lay naked in the stare he gave him. Then, with a single harsh obscenity, he swung away and jerked his head at the men of Stiles's crew, motioning them to their waiting animals.

For the moment it looked as though Tate Corman intended behaving himself. Ben Murdock eased out the breath he had held trapped in his lungs, as all around him leather creaked and riders swung into saddles. Once more the crew of the big Pool herd settled to the routine of getting the drive to stirring, and stretched out in the familiar line of march.

One could believe that last night's storm had been a very local one. By midafternoon there was little sign of it left. Exactly as before, yellow dust, bone-dry as if water had never touched it, rose under the knifing passage of thousands of hoofs, forming a plume that stained the sky for miles. Just as before, the dust fogged a rider's vision, crept into his clothing and through the folds of the neckcloth he pulled up across his nose and mouth. It sent him repeatedly to the water can he carried on his saddle, to swab out a throat grown hoarse with the dust and with yelling into the constant, protesting bellow of the herd.

A very ordinary sort of day, in Ben Murdock's experience.

This Ellsworth trail he was following, which branched west from the Chisholm some miles below in the Indian Nations, had seen travel for only a year or two, but given a few more seasons the passage of herds like this one would have carved out a channel in the surface of the prairie broad enough and deep enough for any Texas cattleman to follow easily all the way from Red River Crossing to the railroad. With a pair of rival lines building across Kansas, almost any town that sprang up along either the Kansas Pacific or the Santa Fe might, like Ellsworth, fancy itself as a terminus for the long drives. One day, of course, Texas would have her own railroads and shipping ports. On that day the long drives would be over, and drovers like Ben Murdock would have to find other work.

Wherever he might go from here, he knew that after a life of distances and dangers—after the challenge of each dawn, and the weight of responsibility that drew a man out fine and tested him a hundred times a day—any other profession was apt to seem tame and unutterably dull by contrast. For now he lived each day as it came. This was his job, and he was good at it. A man took pride in something he did well.

He traveled twice as far in a day as any man of his crew, because he was always ranging up and down the length of the cow column, checking everything, looking to be on hand anywhere an emergency might develop. The dust haze that blotted out the sky did nothing to cut the impact of the sun's fierce heat. By midafternoon a hot west wind had begun to strengthen, its gusts engulfing him in swirls of grit that stung his face and turned his bronc so restive it had to be held in line with a firm hand.

It was at such a moment that he glimpsed a pair of riders waiting in the pall of dust ahead of him. They were Tate Corman and Dab Pollard. They had hauled up and were sitting motionless, and something in the way they watched him approach struck a warning note and turned him cautious. Pulling in, he looked from one to the other. He asked, "Was there something you wanted?"

"From you?" Tate Corman answered harshly. "Not a damn thing!"

The three of them could have been alone here, swallowed by the dust; the herd, only yards away, was almost invisible as it flowed past in a clamor of lowing and cracking ankle joints and clacking horns. Corman's stare was a challenge, unwavering; but when Murdock glanced at his companion he saw how Dab Pollard's look slid back and forth, shifting about as though it couldn't quite decide where it wanted to be. Ben Murdock shrugged and booted the bay horse, starting past them.

But something had his nerves strung tight, and when he heard a whisper of sound behind him he hurriedly twisted around in the saddle. That movement probably saved his life. Tate Corman's gun, pointed at him, looked as big as a cannon and its explosion was a blinding flash, but somehow the bullet missed. Shocked that this man would actually try to kill him, Ben Murdock remembered the sixshooter he'd taken the precaution of digging out and strapping on that morning. Belatedly he started to grope for it—just as a strong gust of the searing wind smote them all broadside, and filled his eyes with grit that stung and instantly blinded him.

Driven by the lash of dust, the tormented bay bolted and Murdock could only let him go. A shout went up behind him as the horse carried him away from there. He had a blurred glimpse of the ground sloping off ahead to a line of drooping cottonwood and scrub, plainly marking a dry watercourse. Then he was clawing at his streaming eyes in a frantic effort to clear them.

Behind him the gun spoke again. In almost the same

instant his horse stumbled briefly and Murdock was thrown violently forward against the saddlehorn. He had enough presence of mind to keep from righting himself. Instead, bobbing loosely, trying to act like a man who had been hit by a bullet, he let the animal carry him on into the shadow of the cottonwoods. They closed over him. The bay leaped down to the litter-strewn floor of the dry streambed, and at once Murdock straightened up and pulled to the right, deeper into the dry course of the wash. After a few yards he found the place he wanted, and sent his animal at the bank.

It dug in its hoofs and went up, sending sand and loose dirt flying. In a clump of brush and timber Murdock drew rein. His gun was in his hand; with the other hand he used his neckcloth to mop dirt and tears from his face, while the horse blew between his knees. His eyes still burned with grit, but by blinking he cleared them well enough to see—and just in time, for here came Corman and Pollard, riding hard in pursuit of the man they no doubt thought they had wounded.

They never saw him as he waited in the shadows with the paper-dry leaves of the trees rustling overhead. They rode down to the edge of the creekbed and there they halted, as though surprised not to find him there. Murdock didn't give them long to wonder about it. A kick of his heel sent the bay forward, coming in behind the pair. He said crisply, "All right, let me see those guns on the ground!"

It was almost comical, the way they froze. Tate Corman half turned, and the man's jaw went slack at the sight of Murdock, plainly unhurt. When he saw there was a gun pointed at him he opened his fist and let his own weapon fall at his horse's feet, whereupon Murdock swung the muzzle of his revolver toward Dab Pollard and the latter, gone suddenly ashen, hastily followed suit.

Murdock again looked coldly at Tate Corman. "Now what's this all about?" he demanded. "Somehow I never figured you wanted my job bad enough to take it by murder!"

The muscles bunched in the man's blunt jaw. "You can go to hell!"

"Very possibly," Ben Murdock agreed, "but I don't aim to let you send me!" He switched his look to the second man. "And you, Pollard. What's *your* trouble— still sore because I showed you up for a tinhorn, and tossed that marked deck into the fire?" He shook his head, studying them both. "If the pair of you hold that kind of grudge, I suppose it's your privilege. But by the same token, I hope you realize there ain't a man would say I wasn't in my rights if I was to go ahead now and finish what you started here!"

Dab Pollard had lost all his smugness. There was all at once a sheen of moisture on his cheeks that was more than the day's heat would have put there. He looked at the gun and his voice cracked slightly as he shouted back, "Then, damn you, go ahead and finish it!"

But Murdock shook his head. "I may be sorry I didn't," he admitted. "But it don't happen to be my style." Deliberately he shoved his gun back into its holster, but kept his hand on it.

He could see the two Stiles men relax slightly; they

exchanged glances, and the relief in Dab Pollard's sallow face was plain. Hot wind rattled the dry branches overhead and raised a swirl of grit that stung the horses' legs and made them move around a little. Murdock settled the bay with the pressure of his knee.

He told his prisoners, "I honestly don't know what to make of you, but whatever the reason, I don't cotton to being shot in the back! I wonder if I'm supposed to believe this was a little something your boss cooked up before he left."

Tate Corman snorted scornfully. "If Stiles wanted someone killed, he wouldn't need it done for him! You just might find that out, if you really got nerve enough to show your face at Ellsworth!"

Murdock's eyes narrowed, but the comment didn't deserve an answer. Wanting only to be gone from there, he lifted the reins. "I've learned one lesson, anyway," he said roughly. "The two of you can bet that from now on I don't make the mistake again of turning my back on you!" He gave the bay a kick and let it carry him past them, up the long slope of prairie toward the slow tide of hides and horns and dust—heading back to his job.

He didn't hurry or look about, confident he'd be beyond range before either Corman or Pollard thought to step down and retrieve the guns he'd made them get rid of.

Sorely troubled as he was, he thought it unlikely anyone else could know what had been going on— until, moments later, he sighted Vern Hoyt spurring toward him along the beef column. Hoyt sang out and, hastily drawing rein, told him, "Ben, somebody said he heard gunshots back this way!"

Murdock kept his face expressionless. "Shots?"

"Two of 'em, he said."

"Is he sure he didn't imagine it?"

Hoyt peered at him narrowly, plainly confused by the trail boss's lack of concern. Pulling off his hat and wiping a sleeve across his forehead, he said hesitantly, "Well, he seemed pretty damned certain. But . . . if *you* say you didn't hear anything—"

"Forget it," Ben Murdock told him shortly, certain that no good would come of letting news of the encounter spread through the trail crew. For his part, Hoyt was clearly less than satisfied, but he fell in beside his boss and together they drifted their horses along the fringe of the slowly moving herd.

Abruptly Vern Hoyt said, "I think I better tell you, things are getting kind of tense since this morning. I mean, with that fellow Stiles pulling out the way he did."

"Stiles? I didn't suppose he was all that popular."

Hoyt made a face. "None of my boys can stand the sonofabitch! But everyone knows he's tough, and he must be capable or the Pool wouldn't have voted him authority to market this herd for them. And at least he usually manages to keep that crew of his in line, if only for the sake of appearances. But now that he's left, some of the boys are worried. They all saw the way Corman defied you the minute his boss was gone."

"He backed down," Murdock pointed out.

"That time, yes. But there's bound to be others. Ben,

Tate Corman hates your guts!"

Murdock scowled into the haze of dust. He could well imagine the reaction he'd get if he were even to hint at what had happened back there by the dry streambed. For a moment he considered taking Vern Hoyt into his confidence, but then decided against it. Hoyt had been alarmed enough already. Corman and Pollard were Murdock's problem, and he would handle it; such problems were part of the burden of command.

The other was continuing, in the same sour tone: "Tate Corman's nothing but trash—him and all his friends, Dab Pollard and that lowlife Jed Finch. But Corman's the worst. He's tough and he's dangerous, and I don't reckon there's a man in the crew that wouldn't admit to being scared of him. I do know that since this morning more than one has got a pistol out of his saddle roll and is wearing it now in the open."

That brought a sharp look from Murdock. "Vern, I will not have this drive turned into an armed camp, for any reason! You tell your boys that."

"Tell Corman!" his friend answered bluntly. "I ain't sure my boys would listen. Not the mood they're in! Ben, there's bad blood in this outfit—I guess you'd call it 'trail fever'—and it's mostly Corman's doing. I can only promise if trouble comes I'll try to see that my boys don't start it!"

"Good enough, Vern," Ben Murdock said quietly. "That's all I ask from you."

Water and grass for the cattle were the main considerations in locating a herd ground for the night. This afternoon George and Rafael had even found some

37

shade to stake out the wagons—a few starved-looking cottonwoods along a meandering stream. The stream was mostly sand and brackish pools, with a sluggish flow of water between its eroded banks. A fire had been built, beans and meat were already in the pans, biscuits in the Dutch oven and coffee boiling in the heavy cast-iron pot when Murdock rode in. Grasshoppers leaped and snapped about his boots as he stepped down into long grass and weeds at the bedroll wagon to see how it was with Wally McKay.

He was alarmed by what he discovered. The hurt man looked out of his head, and feverish with more than the concentration of heat beneath the wagon canvas. The cook told Murdock, "I don't like it a damn bit! One minute he's got the shakes, and the next it's like he's burning up. If you ask me, it come of lying out in that weather last night in a state of shock from the busted leg. I'd say he had him a case of pneumonia." When Murdock nodded solemnly, George added, "Rattling around in this wagon ain't doing him any good at all. What he needs is a bed under him. And a doctor!"

Murdock couldn't argue with that; any puncher who took sick or was hurt on a trail drive was in a desperate way. He left orders for Rafael to fetch water from the creek and keep soaked cloths on the injured man in an effort to cut the fever. Beyond that there was little anyone could do.

Someone had jingled up a fresh mount for him from the remuda. His thoughts were somber as he stripped the fagged animal he'd been riding, switched his gear to the new horse and put it on the picket line against an emergency. That done, he paused to stretch tired back and shoulder muscles as he observed some of his crew moving about the camp.

Something had changed, and he saw at once what it was: Every rider in sight was now openly wearing the handgun he usually carried in his saddle roll.

Vern Hoyt was right, then—things had really deteriorated that much, in less than a day! His attention settled briefly on the cookfire, where a couple of the Box L riders had paused to help themselves to coffee from the big pot. A trio consisting of Jed Finch, Dab Pollard and a second Stiles hand came rolling up, talking loudly and striding the dry grass as though they owned it. Murdock saw a quick reaction from the Box L men: One quietly switched his tin cup from right hand to left, freeing his gun hand; the other, who had been lounging against a wheel of the nearby chuckwagon, quickly straightened.

Both movements were small, but they registered with Pollard and his companions. For just an instant they halted, and an unspoken challenge passed across the fire. Then Finch said something that drew a jeering laugh from his companions, and the three veered aside and moved on. But Murdock had seen enough. It was beginning to look like an armed camp, with Tate Corman and his cronies against the rest.

Vern Hoyt approached. He appeared not to have seen the incident, but he must have read Murdock's expression. He demanded, "What happened?"

"Nothing." But a thought that had been taking shape in his mind suddenly became a decision, and the trail boss asked, "Vern, would you still have the paper you showed me a while back? It was a handbill . . ."

"You mean *this?*" Hoyt brought out of his pocket a folded wad of paper that was damp and crumpled. "Why, you know me—I never throw nothing away."

Ben Murdock took it. "Come along," he said, "I want to talk to Sherm Watkins."

The Pool rancher was giving some instructions to one of his crew. Interrupted, he frowned as he looked at the handbill Murdock offered him. "'Eden Grove, Kansas,'" he read in a dry tone. He gave the trail boss a probing stare. "Yeah, I've seen these; there were quite a number floating around Texas this spring. Somebody's always promoting some new town or other. Mostly I imagine they're only on paper—or in the heads of the men who put out the circulars."

According to the promoters of this one, Eden Grove would have to be the boomingest city in the entire West. There was a map showing its location on the banks of the Arkansas, and the future line of the Atchison, Topeka and Santa Fe following up the river's course. Eden Grove, the flier stated without undue modesty, was certain to become the metropolis of western Kansas, a shipping point commanding the trade in Texas cattle. Sherm Watkins handed the circular back. "So what about it?"

"By my figuring," Murdock said, "we'll hit the Arkansas tomorrow, with another two full days' drive to Ellsworth. I propose that we not cross the river, but bear west and bring the herd in to Eden Grove instead."

Watkins stared. "Not go on to Ellsworth? Are you serious?"

"I don't need to tell you that knocking a couple of days off the drive can put money in your pocket. What concerns me even more, though, is that man in the wagon. One more day of this is just about all he can take. It looks now as though he's developed pneumonia. He's got to have a doctor."

"And what makes you think you'll find one at this Eden Grove? How do you know we'll even find a town?"

"I don't claim to know anything, except that it's the only hope for saving Wally McKay!"

The cowman scowled, unable to answer that argument. Vern Hoyt, who had been keeping silent, spoke up. "I reckon you'll at least find your town. Remember them two punchers that stopped to share camp with us last week? They was trailing south after taking a herd to Wichita. Well, I learned talking to them that the Santa Fe's building up the Arkansas right on schedule, hopes to reach Fort Dodge before snow flies. As for Eden Grove, I understand they even got them a newspaper."

Watkins gave a grunt of skepticism. "A newspaper don't make a town! Ben," he told Murdock, "the Pool contracted with you to make this drive to Ellsworth, not anywhere else."

"Not true, Sherm. I signed to deliver a herd; that was all. If Eden Grove turns out to be nothing then we'll drop Wally McKay off, for whatever help he can find there, and take the cattle on to Ellsworth. We'll lose

41

nothing, and for all we know we just might save those two days I mentioned."

"You're forgetting Wilson Stiles! Marketing this beef is his job, and he's headed for Ellsworth."

Hoyt answered that. "So we get a rider off, let him know about the change of plans."

A muscle worked in the cowman's cheek as he considered Ben Murdock's expression. "All right, Ben," he said finally with a nod. "I'm not sure you're telling me everything. But I backed you so far. If it's really that important, I'll back you now."

"Thanks," Murdock said. "It's that important."

Sherm Watkins lifted his shoulders. "Then I better find Jed Finch and let him know what's happening. He'll probably buck like hell, but I can handle him."

Watching him stomp away, Vern Hoyt said dryly, "There goes a worried man! One place I think he guessed right—you *ain't* telling him everything!"

"You think not?"

"I know it!" Hoyt gave the trail boss a chance to respond, and when Murdock didn't answer he added, "I'm wondering if you've stopped to think what Tate Corman and his friends might say about it."

Murdock looked at him. "Suppose you tell me."

"When Wilson Stiles pulled out he was making talk about seeing you later, at Ellsworth. I wouldn't put it past them two to go spreading it around how Wally McKay is only your excuse to get out of facing Stiles—how you figure to dump this herd at Eden Grove and run for it!"

"Do *you* think I'm afraid to face Stiles?"

42

"Nobody could be blamed for acting careful with him. But *afraid?*" Hoyt spat into the dry weeds. "Hell, I wouldn't think you'd have to ask me!"

"Thanks. All the same I wouldn't like being pushed into a showdown, because I can't see any sense to it, or any cause." He hesitated. "But to be honest with you, something else is beginning to worry me—the odds on my being able to hold this outfit together the rest of the way to Ellsworth. You tried to warn me, Vern, and you were right. It's turned into an armed camp!"

Vern Hoyt nodded slowly, his sun-weathered face sober. "I see. *That's* what you didn't tell Sherm Watkins! That's the reason you want to cut the drive short at Eden Grove, before it has time to blow!"

"It's part of the reason," the other agreed. "Like I told Sherm, though, Wally McKay is the main part."

"Of course. . . ." For a moment neither spoke. Suddenly a dry chuckle broke from Vern Hoyt and got him a quick look from Murdock.

"Something funny?"

"Not really," Hoyt said, shaking his head. "It just occurred to me: Those people at Eden Grove will likely break out a celebration tomorrow when they see a herd this size making for their shipping pens. But when they find out what else we're bringing 'em, they may cuss the fact they ever laid eyes on this outfit!"

Ben Murdock had no answer for that.

CHAPTER III

As he descended the steps to the hotel lobby, Mayor
Steadman saw the man in the open doorway, silhou-
etted against the blast of light outside. A questioning
look got a confirming nod from his nephew, Barney
Osgood, who had summoned him. Barney returned to
whatever he was occupied with behind the desk, and
Steadman advanced to meet the stranger.

While waiting, bowler hat in hand, the man had been
looking out over Railroad Avenue, past the shimmering
tracks and the box-like depot to the row of buildings, at
various stages of construction, that lined the wide
street's south side. Before he spoke Steadman had a
moment to observe his features in repose. He saw a
face that appeared naturally solemn, with something
almost ascetic about the deepset eyes, and with a mouth
that was bracketed deeply by lines carved into the flat
cheeks. It might have been a scholar's face, and Phil
Steadman only hoped his own face didn't reveal his
surprise. "Good afternoon," he said pleasantly, and
held out a hand. "I'm Phil Steadman."

Every movement the other made seemed deliberate,
and performed with a spare economy. This showed in
the way he turned his head, the brooding eyes studying
the hotelman for an instant before he acknowledged the
greeting with a slight nod. Taking the hand, he said,
"Gerringer."

"So the boy told me," Steadman said, indicating

44

Barney Osgood, who was watching with undisguised interest from behind the lobby desk. "I've been hoping for some word from you, Mr. Gerringer. I just wasn't expecting you'd come in person."

Jay Gerringer gave a slight shrug, lifting a shoulder of the neatly cut box coat he wore despite the heat. "The best place to look a situation over is generally on the ground. I got off the cars a couple of hours ago."

"And you've been looking us over?"

"As much as there was to see."

The mayor of Eden Grove allowed himself a smile. "We're a very small town," he admitted. "But we grow. New businesses opening every week." He added briskly, "Why don't we have us a little drink while we talk?"

The other appeared to find that satisfactory. Steadman ordered his nephew to keep an eye on Gerringer's carpetbag, placed on the floor just inside the hotel entrance, and took his guest through an inner door and into the room that served as his office.

The hotel, like the town, was new and the office sparely furnished, with no carpet on the pine flooring. Steadman offered one of the two barrel chairs and settled into the other one behind the desk, where he took out a bottle and glasses and poured drinks for them both. The warm air flowing through an open window carried scents of dust and scorched grass, and the muted sounds of the village. They could hear a saw and hammer at work somewhere, and the sounds of busy housekeeping activities within the big, two-storied hotel itself.

Phil Steadman looked over the rim of his glass at the other man, still hard put to match Gerringer's appearance with his reputation as a law officer. "So you're Jay Gerringer!" he began. "Somehow I expected . . ."

"Yes?" the other prompted.

He shook his head. "Come to think of it, I don't really know what I expected. After all, what kind of man chooses your line of work?"

"As many kinds, I suppose, as choose any other. What sort of a man becomes a hotelkeeper?"

That was a valid question, and Steadman found an answer. "Ordinarily, he ain't one you'd expect to strap on a gun and go out to face a drunken railroad hand or some other threat to the peace!"

Jay Gerringer merely smiled, an expression that made his watchful eyes seem even more aloof. Somehow the smile put an end to that line of conversation; it seemed to say: *What kind of man I am is something you'll have to decide for yourself!* Phil Steadman let it go. He lifted the bottle, offering to pour again, but Gerringer shook his head and Steadman set the whiskey aside. The other man suggested, "Shall we discuss the job you've offered me? To begin with, the price is a little low, but I'm assuming that can be negotiated."

Steadman hesitated; salary was a touchy subject. "I want to be clear," he said finally, toying with his empty shot glass. "It wasn't exactly an offer—not yet. You understand that we have a town council that has to make any final decisions; when I wrote, it was only to find out if you'd be open to a bid. Now that you're here, the obvious thing would be to meet with the council and let them look you over. And they can answer any questions you might have."

"Suits me," Gerringer said. "When does this happen?"

"In just about"—the hotelman pulled out a gold watch the size of a silver dollar and thumbed open the case—"twenty minutes. We hold our regular weekly meeting at two o'clock." He snapped the watch shut and put it back in his trousers. "As to the price . . . well, I hope you understand just how new a town we are! We've been incorporated less than a month; the Santa Fe brought its rails through barely a week ago. We've been hoping to draw some of the Texas trail herds, but the first one's still to arrive. Truth is, we're marking time at the moment, and there isn't an awful lot of money in the till. Very soon we expect to do much better."

Gerringer's mouth tilted skeptically. "You seem to be building chiefly on expectations."

"Every new town has to."

"But can you actually afford the kind of law you're thinking about? Are you even sure you need it?" Gerringer gestured toward the window, indicating the peaceful sounds of industry carried in on the warm breeze from outside. "Things seem quiet enough."

"For how long?" Phil Steadman replied. "Abilene was quiet enough, too—until the Texas trade blew it wide open. We think Eden Grove is the logical successor, now that Abilene's taken herself out of the market. After all, we're forty miles closer than

Ellsworth, and we're west of the Texas fever quarantine line, which gives us an edge on Newton and Wichita. But unlike them we mean to clamp a lid on lawbreaking, not give it a chance to get out of hand the way it seems to have done at those other places. We've had homicides already—too many; three, by last count, along with a couple of incidents that just missed turning into killings. Violence at Eden Grove is as old as the town itself. In fact, right now we've got a man in the county jail at Hutchinson, waiting trial for a murder he committed here before there was so much as a single building."

"Oh?" The deepset eyes studied him. "Is there a story in that?"

"I suppose. Nat Colby and his partner were the ones who originally laid out the town and platted it, a year ago. Lately, by accident, we learned that the two of them murdered and robbed a man who happened by. He was a gambler, and it was money they found on him they used in building and promoting Eden Grove. They were doing well at it, too, until something tripped them up.

"But now we're rid of them both, and a group of the town's honest businessmen have the reins. We're negotiating for a loan with a bank in Kansas City, to assume the assets the partnership still held when the law caught up with them. Virg Beason was killed resisting arrest, and Colby hasn't much choice left but to sell—fighting that murder charge will take every dollar he can raise. Oh, they were a choice pair of crooks, all right! It's a good thing to be rid of them."

Phil Steadman slapped his knees with both palms, then, and rose. "Getting near two o'clock," he said. "We'd better go."

The unpainted wooden building where Eden Grove's council met had been the original townsite company office. It stood alone at the eastern end of Railroad Avenue, five blocks over, near a clump of dusty cottonwoods that had been the source of a name for the village. As the meandering footpath took Steadman and his guest in that direction, past empty intersections and vacant lots broken by a mere scatter of raw new business structures, they encountered at most some two dozen people: townsmen who stood staring in their doorways or came out to be introduced to the stranger; a couple of farmers in off their homestead claims with wagon and team to pick up a few supplies. They saw one noisy clutch of railroad hands, off shift and making a tour of the street's three saloons, but altogether there was not much activity and Phil Steadman felt called on to offer a comment:

"You might not think it to look at us, but a few weeks back this place was boiling over with boomers and speculators, all hoping to make a killing. That's done now, and they've drifted on and left it to those of us who actually care about having a permanent town here.

"There's some may be disappointed that things don't move any faster, particularly because we haven't begun yet to reap our share of the Texas trade. That's all right.

We are a little west of the main drive routes, but sooner or later somebody's going to find out we got a railroad and shipping pens waiting. Let that news get onto the grapevine and we'll see more activity than we may know how to deal with!"

The other man listened but held his tongue.

Steadman and Gerringer were the last to arrive for the meeting. As they approached the squat frame building they found three others on the steps waiting. This was the town government *pro tem,* appointed when the court accepted Eden Grove's petition for organization under Kansas statute, and Mayor Steadman introduced them: John Riggs, the town doctor; Clark Tanner, who owned and edited the Eden Grove *Gazette*; and a gaunt, bearded man named Tom McDougall, operator of the local livery. "Jim Lawless won't be here," the mayor said. "He told me yesterday he had to go into Hutchinson on some matter. But we're a quorum. We'll proceed without him."

Though they all knew Steadman had written to sound out Jay Gerringer about taking the marshal's job, they were obviously as surprised as he to see the man arrive like this—in person, unannounced. Tom McDougall sounded a note of suspicion as he said bluntly, "I wouldn't have thought you could get away from your job to come here. Or maybe you're not working at the moment?"

That got him a slow look before Gerringer answered, "No. As a matter of fact, I'm not."

"I see." McDougall glanced at the mayor with an expression that said plainly, *You didn't tell us this!*

Steadman, irritated, ignored the man and led the way into the office.

It was virtually as its former occupants, Beason and Colby, had left it—a few straight-backed chairs, a couple of desks beyond a divider railing, a safe, and on one wall a map of Eden Grove with the sale of building lots marked on it in ink. As mayor, Phil Steadman took his place behind one of the desks and the others drew up chairs for themselves. John Riggs opened the discussion, peering at the stranger through the lenses of his steel-rimmed spectacles. "I suppose," the doctor said, "Phil has been giving you the situation here."

"I have," said Steadman.

"Then we can skip the preliminaries. We are men who all have faith in this town," the doctor told Gerringer solemnly. "We have an idea of the place we'd like it to be. We also know just what we *don't* want—a wide-open cattle town, like certain others I don't have to name. We hope you can help us avoid that."

Jay Gerringer took his time in answering. He seemed completely at ease under their scrutiny—chair tilted on its back legs, thumbs in waistcoat pockets, bowler on his knee. "You're right to be concerned," he said finally, "and not taken by surprise the way those other towns were. But I can't guarantee miracles."

Clark Tanner said, "No one expects miracles."

"I hope not. A peace officer is only as effective as the support he gets. Too often there are elements that *want* a wide-open town, or so they tell themselves. They think it means bigger profits."

The newspaperman nodded soberly. "You may find

51

that element. We'll help you deal with it the best we can."

Gerringer appeared to consider the remark, while the others watched him—all, Phil Steadman thought, attempting to read the man to their satisfaction. "Where would I be headquartered?" the lawman asked.

"We thought, right here," Steadman answered, indicating the building where they sat. "For the time being. You may have noticed we don't have a jail as yet. So far we've been lucky enough to get by without one. As I told you, we're short of funds but we have the lot set aside, and we hope to get something built very soon now."

"You had better build it soon," Gerringer remarked flatly. "And build it stout!"

"Agreed," Steadman answered.

"I'm told," Clark Tanner put in, "that the first jail they built at Abilene, the Texans came in and tore it apart. . . ."

The mayor looked about him. "Well, are there any more questions? From anyone?"

Tom McDougall said, "I've got a question."

"Oh?" Steadman kept his face expressionless. Knowing McDougall's quarrelsome nature, he could judge from the liveryman's tone that they might be in for a fight. "All right, Tom, let's hear it."

"It's about you getting fired, at Leavenworth some months back. There's been conflicting stories, Gerringer, and I'm a little confused. I'd like you to tell us exactly what happened."

"It was in all the papers," Tanner reminded him.

McDougall gave the editor a cold look. "Newspapers

52

are *your* business. I ain't got much time for them."

Jay Gerringer showed no emotion as he answered the question. "What happened at Leavenworth was simple enough. A few of the town's merchants got together to fix prices and gouge the soldiers from the fort. If they'd asked me I could have told them it would lead to trouble. When the trouble came, they expected me to pull it out of the fire for them."

"I understood there was a riot," McDougall interrupted.

"Riot?" Gerringer shrugged. "If that's what you'd call a couple dozen soldiers with a grudge against being cheated. Two business places had some damage before I was able to stop it, but I refused to make any arrests or collect damages—that was up to the military. What's more, I considered the businessmen who got hurt had brought it on themselves."

"The Leavenworth authorities didn't see it that way," the liveryman snapped. "They fired you!"

A flash of wry humor deepened a corner of the other's mouth. "You could say I was given to understand my resignation would be accepted."

"I fail to see the difference!" Tom McDougall said stiffly.

The humor vanished. "I didn't mean to suggest that there was one," Gerringer replied.

Clark Tanner made an impatient gesture. "We're talking in circles. This is all ancient history anyway. We have a decision to make. Can we take a vote and settle it?"

"Not yet!" McDougall told him. "First, I want this

man to leave the room for a few minutes."

"Oh, for the love of—!" John Riggs started to exclaim, but Gerringer was already getting to his feet in the spare, uncluttered way he had of moving. "It's all right," he said. "I could use a little fresh air." Though the windows were open and the double doors propped back, there was very little breeze to stir the breathless heat of August. Watching Gerringer step outside into the blast of the sun, Steadman was aware of a trickle of sweat across his own ribs. He turned back impatiently to the others on the town council.

"Well, Tom," he said to McDougall, "let's have it. What bothers you?"

"It doesn't bother *you?*" the latter retorted. "Here's a town officer who admits he let a bunch of drunken soldiers run wild, and then sided with them against the men who paid his wages. And what he did once, he could do again."

"I don't think I'd worry too much," Clark Tanner said with a faint smile. "The nearest troops are at Fort Larned, and that's thirty miles away."

McDougall looked at him with ice in his stare. "I suppose that was meant for a joke! Let me tell you, we could wish they were closer if we once get a few hundred Johnny Reb trailhands loose in this town, and find we have a marshal who doesn't bother to keep them under control!"

" 'Johnny Rebs,' " Doc Riggs murmured, and looked up at a corner of the ceiling. "You still fighting the War, Tom? I thought it was seven years over. . . ."

McDougall ignored the comment. He turned toward

Phil Steadman. "Didn't it occur to you to wonder why the man's out of a job? With his record, what town would hire him! I'll wager anything he's flat broke—or why was he desperate enough to come running out here, on nothing stronger than a query? Why is he trying his damnedest to sell himself to us?"

There was an uneasy silence as they considered that. Outside in the bright sunlight they could see Jay Gerringer talking to a horseman who had just ridden up, man and mount and gear all bearing the stains of hard travel, trail dust clinging to the sweaty hide of the bay horse and to the wide brim of the hat that shielded the rider's face.

Clark Tanner said, "Look at it from this angle: Tom may have an argument; on the other hand, if the man's really that much in need of a job, he could be just as anxious not to risk losing it. Who's to say he hasn't learned a lesson?"

"That's right!" John Riggs asserted, the steel-rimmed spectacles flashing with the vigor of his nod. "Besides, where can we hope to get any other man of his caliber for the amount we're able to pay? If anything, this is a lucky break for Eden Grove. We had better grab it."

"I agree." Steadman looked at the livery owner. "Tom?"

Tom McDougall, scowling, rubbed the knuckles of one hand across his short-bearded jaw and shrugged. "I'm out-voted—that's clear. But I insist, this has to be on a trial basis. It's up to the man to prove himself."

"You could say the same about the town," Doc Riggs commented. "Go call him in, Phil."

When he heard his name, Gerringer broke off talking to the strange rider and followed the mayor back inside. He stood at the gate in the railing partition, bowler in one hand, his face expressionless as he awaited the verdict. Steadman gave it to him quickly. "I guess the job is yours if you care to try it—shall we say, for a month? I'm afraid the pay will have to be as stated, at least to begin with: eighty dollars and fees."

Jay Gerringer hesitated before he nodded agreement. "In advance." At that, Tom McDougall looked around at his fellow council members as though to say, *I told you he was broke!*

"Come with me," the mayor said, "and I'll get your money. We also have a badge for you. Will you be able to start at once?"

The new marshal nodded again. "And that might not be too soon! You've got a man waiting outside with five thousand head of Texas longhorns, in mixed brands, pointed at your stockpens."

"What!" Clark Tanner was on his feet. "Did you say five thousand—in a single herd?"

"And a thirty-man crew, one of them bad hurt. The trail boss came on ahead to find a doctor for him, and somebody down the street told him to try here. So, gentlemen, it looks as though your town of Eden Grove is suddenly in the cattle business. I wish you luck!"

CHAPTER IV

Ben Murdock had been able to get only a jumbled impression of Eden Grove—the dazzling smear of the Santa Fe tracks, a wide and dusty street, a scatter of unpainted, raw-lumber buildings under a white-hot August sky. His concerns were too urgent to let him notice more. Luckily, the first anxious queries about a doctor had paid off: The bald and sweating fat man who lounged in the door of the New York Restaurant, a dishtowel apron tied about his immense middle, sensed the emergency and wasted no words as he pointed out the building where, he said, John Riggs would be sitting in a meeting of the city council.

Murdock's reception there, with his news that five thousand head of Texas longhorns would be pouring onto the Arkansas River flats sometime before sundown, was like a bombshell going off. He was scarcely given time to sort out faces, or to handle a barrage of questions. But his insistence on the need for help for Wally McKay finally got results. A quiet-eyed, competent man named Steadman, who had been introduced as the mayor of Eden Grove, shunted aside the talk to ask, "Where have you got this hurt cowboy?"

"He's with the wagons, not too far behind me. We'll be setting up camp on the flats, the other side of the river."

"You brought him to the right place; there's not a better doctor in the state of Kansas than John Riggs. We don't want to waste any time, John. You'd best go and see what needs to be done."

In less than a half hour after his arrival, Murdock was riding out again, accompanied by the doctor with the grizzled mustache and the steel-rimmed spectacles. Riggs had borrowed a flatbed and team from McDougall to convey the injured trailhand to his own office in town if that should be necessary. He carried a passenger with him, a homely young man, about Murdock's age, who had also been at the meeting—Clark Tanner, who owned and edited the town's newspaper. He seemed to be troubled by a bad leg that gave him a limp and obviously bothered him as he climbed up to the wagon's hard seat.

They left a town that was already stirring, reacting to the news of an approaching trail herd rather like an ant hill that has been poked with a stick. But the most impressive image Murdock took away from there was the somber face of the man named Gerringer—the brooding stare directed at the Texan, while in the background the voice of the sour-faced stable owner said to no one in particular, "Looks as though we might have a chance, right off, to see what kind of a marshal we've had wished off on us. Nothing like a bunch of wild-eyed Texas trailhands for putting him to the test!"

Ben Murdock somehow had the feeling he was being hurled at Gerringer's head, and he didn't much like it. The last thing he wanted, he thought as he gave the bay a touch of his heel, was to see himself and the Pool herd inadvertently caught in a morass of small-time village politics.

Buffalo hoofs, and the unshod horses of the Indians who for centuries had roamed this land, had cut the trail that led across the flats to where a shallowing of the riverbed, braided with sand bars, made a natural crossing. When Murdock had splashed across he pulled in briefly to let the doctor's rig catch up to him, then pointed southward through the shimmer of heatwaves on sun-browned grass and called back over a shoulder, "There's the wagons now."

George had found a place where there was sufficient wood and water, and he had the chuckwagon tailgate lowered and a fire built and was up to his elbows in biscuit dough when he saw the group arriving from the direction of town. He gave a shout for Rafael, who came running to hold the half-wild livery team while John Riggs and the crippled newspaper editor got down. In answer to Murdock's questions, the Mexican youth could report little change in Wally McKay as he led the visitors to the bedroll wagon.

The canvas had been rolled up, but the heat trapped under it was stifling. Crawling in beside the hurt puncher, Murdock couldn't tell whether it was the sickness or the filtered light that gave McKay's skin its sallow look.

With professional efficiency, Riggs set about his examination—testing the puncher's temperature, counting his pulse, rolling back the lids for a look at his eyes. He nodded soberly. "You've got a pretty sick man here."

"Pneumonia?"

"No question about it." Riggs checked the splints on

the broken leg and said, "At least, whoever set that did a good job; it doesn't appear to have slipped. . . . Nothing I can do for him here," the doctor added. "Let's get him into the flatbed. I'll take him to my place and put him to bed where I can keep an eye on him."

Murdock said, "I'll ask George and Rafael to lend a hand."

They discovered there had been a new arrival in camp while they were busy at the wagon. Sherm Watkins, unable to wait longer, had left the herd and ridden on ahead to get a look at the place to which the Pool herd had been driven against his better judgment. As soon as Clark Tanner learned the identity of the Pool owner, he lost no time in cornering Watkins and pumping him for information. Watkins was answering his questions impatiently but Murdock sensed he was flattered, too. Coming up on them, Murdock said, "You're in the hands of the press now, Sherm. Maybe you don't realize it, but we're just as important to these people as they and their town are to us." He introduced Riggs, and the doctor repeated what he had said about the sick man in the wagon.

Bruskly, Watkins said, "Let's not stand here talking, then. Let's get him moved."

The transfer was quickly done. Wally McKay roused once and feverishly protested being moved, then subsided. When he had been made comfortable for the brief run into town, Riggs mounted to the seat. Tanner had been invited to stay and watch the herd arrive but he didn't have time. He had a major story to write, and the paper's first page form had to be torn out and reset

60

before he could go to press. He'd gathered all the material he could use for now, he said. He took his place beside Riggs and in a moment the flatbed was tooling away across the flat and toward the jumble of unpainted wooden buildings across the river.

Watching them go, Sherm Watkins said, "Well, you've had a look at Eden Grove. How does it stack up?"

"About as we expected," Murdock told him. "There's not an awful lot to the town as yet, but they've got all the facilities we're looking for, including the rails and the loading pens. From what I was told we'll be the first to use them."

"What's more to the point, did you see any beef money?"

Murdock hesitated. He had known this question was coming, and had debated his answer. "To be honest with you," he admitted, "I didn't. We had some discussion of that. I was told there aren't actually any buyers on the ground, because up to now there's been no business for them. But the mayor insisted he's got commission houses and independent dealers interested. We show him the beef, and he tells me he only has to send off a couple of telegrams to bring us the buyers."

Watkins frowned. "And how long is this supposed to take?"

"He said a day or two at the longest."

The other was plainly none too satisfied. He stroked the leathery flesh of his cheeks as he considered. "I guess it will have to do," he said finally. "We'll just hope to hell your man knows what he's talking about!"

"You can talk to him yourself. The mayor's name is Steadman; he runs the hotel. And if we do have to wait," Murdock pointed out, "it at least gives us time to send word and fetch Wilson Stiles back from Ellsworth."

"Yeah . . . there's that, I guess."

Though the Pool owner was still unconvinced, Ben Murdock could see no further use in standing there talking. Turning away, he said, "Well, right now I got a herd to meet and keep moving, if we want them on the bedground and settled by nightfall. . . ."

He struck south, leaving the Arkansas bottoms and searching the sun-shot prairie sky ahead for a tawny stain that would be the dust of the approaching herd.

He saw it sooner than he expected. The drive had picked up speed, the trail-weary longhorns somehow seeming to know that the weeks of endless plodding were nearly over. The rangy beasts came shambling on over the sun-cured grass to the accompaniment of a steady, mournful bawling and the rumble of thousands of hoofs. A couple of horsemen broke away from the drive and spurred ahead to meet the returning trail boss.

They were Vern Hoyt and Ed Qualen, with a dozen anxious questions that Murdock answered as patiently as he could. Was there really a town ahead? What did it look like? Had he been able to find a doctor? He assured them on all counts, and Qualen went spurring back to pass the word. "We're making good time," Murdock told Hoyt as they watched the vanguard of the herd approach, with a big, battle-scarred veteran of other drives—a brindle steer with one horn missing—

leading them. "It's almost as though they smell the river."

"Maybe they do," the other man said. "Maybe that's why they're stepping out so smart. They're anxious as we are to get this over!"

Moving back along the drive, Murdock found that the news Qualen had carried had raised spirits dulled by long and wearing routine, and filled the crew with anticipation. Bad feelings that had threatened to split this outfit seemed held in abeyance. Even Tate Corman, riding with his friend Jed Finch, forgot his enmity long enough to yell at Murdock, almost jovially, "I hear you been and checked out the new town for us. Did you see any women?"

"I didn't look for them," Murdock said without slowing his horse. "But if they're there, I don't doubt you'll find them."

Corman laughed loudly in reply, and Finch allowed himself a raffish snigger. But as Murdock rode past there was no real humor in the cold stare directed at him from the corner of Tate Corman's eye.

The rivalries and resentments hadn't gone anywhere. They were still there, still doing their work, still promising trouble that would come in its own good time.

There was no fanfare when the leaders broke down over the low bluff, and brought the big Pool herd to the end of the long trek north. A low sun hung red and swollen, gilding the dust pall that began to settle as the herd poured out upon the Arkansas bottoms. By the time the cattle had spread out there, the sky was losing its color and taking on a steely hue matched by the metallic sheen of the river.

After a final check Murdock rode over to the wagons and found considerable activity. The remuda had been driven up and riders were roping fresh mounts for the last short mile to the river crossing and the buildings huddled invitingly on the other bank. A few punchers who still had clean shirts in their warbags were breaking them out and shaking the wrinkles from them. Boots were being rubbed up; hair and whiskers that had not been touched since the drive began were getting hacked with scissors and straight-edged razors, amid loud brags about the speed with which the town of Eden Grove would be drunk stone dry, when this crew rode in.

The trail boss listened to them, amused. He then noticed that Sherm Watkins had come out from town to watch the camp being set up. Wanting his opinion of Eden Grove, Murdock rode over and dismounted near the wagons where the Pool owner was conferring with George, the cook. Watkins admitted to being fairly well impressed, but he was still skeptical about the lack of buyers. "I looked up the mayor," he said gruffly. "That fellow Steadman. He's wired Wichita and Kansas City and he swears it will get results. Meanwhile I sent a telegram of my own—to Stiles at Ellsworth. Steadman says they've got two hotels up there, so I'm trying them both and I only hope it reaches him. If he don't show, we can always send off a rider."

Yes, he had looked in on Wally McKay. The doctor had got him into a bed in his office and seemed to be taking good care of him. But Riggs said it was still too early to tell how severe the pneumonia would prove to be. McKay had a fever and it hadn't yet leveled off.

After some further discussion of the herd and its disposition, Murdock spoke a word to George, who obliged him by catching up a saucepan and mixing spoon and raising a clatter with them that brought him everyone's attention. George pointed the spoon at Murdock. "Boss wants to say something. . . ."

Looking them over and gauging their temper, Murdock read a respectful attention in most of the crew, but in others a definite hostility. He saw Tate Corman and Dab Pollard watching him in an attitude of open defiance as they waited to learn what orders he might have for them now. He said into the waiting stillness, "It looks like we've done what we set out to. Far as I ever heard, this has been the largest single bunch of Texas cattle ever to make it up the Chisholm. Our losses have been light, and except for Wally McKay, who's now in the hands of a competent doctor, no rider has even had a serious injury. And that's a record we can be proud of!

"Right now, I know you all want to get over to that town across the river and do some celebrating—even if it ain't precisely the town we thought we were headed for when we left Texas. But it happens we've still got five thousand longhorns that we're responsible for. *They* don't know this is the finish. They've got grass and water here, but they're trail-restless, and unless they're kept together, by morning we could find them strung out for miles along the river bottoms.

"I figure eight men can handle them tonight. And I'm authorized by Sherm Watkins to offer an extra week's wages as a bonus to those who are willing to pass up this first night in town. The boys who are out on the herd now have volunteered to stand the first trick; I'm going to need five more. Let's see some hands."

He looked over the group. He could understand a man's reluctance to give up the celebration he had been looking forward to during all those hard and weary miles. Still, an extra week's wages was a strong inducement. After a moment, four hands went up, one by one. Murdock called off the names, thanking each man in turn. "I need one more." But it seemed there were to be no more volunteers.

"All right," Murdock said after the men had exchanged looks but no additional hands were lifted. "I guess we've got no choice but to draw straws for it. Short man stays, and collects the bonus. . . ." He turned to Vern Hoyt. "Find something we can use."

There was an oath. He had been aware of Tate Corman aggressively eyeing him. Now Corman made a slicing gesture with one hard palm as he exclaimed, "The hell with your bonus, Murdock, and the hell with drawing straws! You want somebody riding herd tonight? Do it yourself! Nobody here takes your orders any longer. You said it yourself—you was hired to rod this drive. But the drive is finished."

"The *job* isn't," Murdock reminded him. "Not until the herd changes hands and a buyer takes over. And as long as there's work still remaining, every man is going to pull his share of it. Let me have those, Vern."

Hoyt had returned with the sticks he had gathered and snapped to the proper lengths. "There's one for everybody," he said. "And one's shorter than the rest."

"Drop them in your hat."

Wordlessly Vern Hoyt took off his battered Stetson, put the sticks into it and shook them up. The trail boss, his eyes never quitting their challenging regard of Corman, said sharply, "All right, Tate. You get first draw."

He was pushing hard, and he knew it, but he had taken as much from Corman as he could afford to without endangering his own authority. Murdock would never forget the bullet at his back that had clearly been intended to kill him. If this was the time to learn if Tate Corman was willing to face him in a show-down, then he was ready. Corman appeared nearly ready himself. He looked at the hat, and his heavy features took on a muddy redness as the angry blood rushed into his cheeks and his fingers clenched and unclenched. Murdock waited, watching his eyes; the signal, if it came, would appear there.

But then Ed Qualen spoke up, his voice shaking with anxiety as the words tumbled over one another in his haste to get them out: "Boss, I guess I can use a week's pay. I'll stay with the herd tonight."

The interruption caught Murdock completely off guard, too absorbed by the expected break with Tate Corman to take it in. When he turned on the puncher, something in the hardness of his stare must have jolted Qualen and made him stammer, as though to justify himself, "I mean . . . only real reason I wanted to ride into town was to see for myself how Wally McKay is doing. But if you say he's in good hands . . ."

"You satisfied, Murdock?" Corman's voice jarred at the trail boss. "Looks like you got your volunteer—and we've had enough of this nonsense!"

The big man's relief at this face-saving turn of events was plain to read, though he tried to hide it with a sneer. He swung away, telling his crew loudly, "Come on, boys, get saddled!" Murdock watched him swagger off, then drew a breath, trying to force the tension from his nerves but feeling strung out and unsatisfied. Beside him, Vern Hoyt muttered something to himself as he shook the unused sticks from his hat and drew it on.

Still, Ed Qualen's intentions had been good, and Murdock was careful to thank the puncher for what he had done. "You may have prevented something pretty bad from happening. Corman was spoiling for a fight, but it was the wrong time for one—not in front of the whole crew."

Vern Hoyt said darkly, "Looks to me the showdown's only been put off awhile. Tate's bound and determined to have it."

"But with luck," Murdock replied, "I can at least pick the moment. . . ."

The moment of departure was drawing near. Sherm Watkins, representing the owners, got out the metal cash box holding the Pool's funds, which had been stowed away in the back of the cookwagon. Using a barrel for a seat and the wagon's tailgate as a desk, he opened the day book in front of him and prepared to pay off the members of the crew. Each man would receive a month's wages of what he had coming, and collect the balance after the herd was sold.

Ben Murdock had a thought that sent him over there, and he shouldered his way through the men crowding up to get their money. Confronting Watkins, he told the cowman, "Sherm, I realize that what these men do on their own time, and away from the herd, is not my responsibility. But don't you think you should give orders that they're to take off their guns and leave them in camp?"

He was not surprised at the dissension he provoked among the men clotted around the wagon. One or two openly hooted at him, and he recognized Dab Pollard's voice saying loudly, "Hell, Murdock! Don't you never quit?"

Murdock ignored them as he pursued his argument. "Nobody's going to need a gun, but with a few drinks under their belts they might be forgetting. Meanwhile, the people in that town have mostly never seen a trail crew. Do we want to risk giving a bad impression?"

Sherm Watkins fiddled with his stub of pencil. "You're probably right," he was saying when Dab Pollard thrust others out of the way and confronted him, a hand clamped to the butt of the revolver in his holster. "Let me tell you this!" he shouted. There was pure malevolence in the glare he directed at Watkins and at Ben Murdock. "The only man that can give me that kind of an order is my boss, and neither of you looks like Wilson Stiles to me!" He thrust out a palm, insolently waggling the fingers under Sherm Watkins' nose. "So quit talking about taking my gun, and fork over my pay. I'm spoiling to find me a poker game, and I need a stake!"

Somebody retorted sourly, "Ain't you got enough of a stake, Pollard? What you cleaned off the rest of us?" The cardsharp acted as if he didn't hear.

Murdock was watching Sherm Watkins, and noticed how the cowman had reddened as he pulled away from the hand shoved into his face. He was a well-intentioned man, but in a moment of pressure there was an indecisiveness about him. Ben Murdock shook his head, knowing someone of stronger will might have imposed his authority. Watkins was not the man to do that, nor would he give Murdock the necessary backing to take over himself and fill the void of leadership. With a shrug the trail boss said curtly, "I guess you may as well pay them," and turned away before he could see the triumph reflected in Dab Pollard's mocking grin.

He rejoined Vern Hoyt and they stood by in moody silence as Watkins continued with the payoffs, counting out the money from the cash box and making notations in his book. As one by one the crew got their pay, there was a rush for the picket line and a noisy departure from camp, riders whooping and yelling in high spirits. Once or twice a gun was unlimbered, its report cracking flatly against the wide expanse of the sky. Watching them spur their horses toward the river crossing, Murdock couldn't help but see how even now the two factions held themselves strictly apart, each man keeping with his friends and pointedly ignoring the others. He didn't like it, and told his companion gruffly, "I remember you tried to warn me I'd not be doing the town any favor, turning this crew loose on it. Get them drinking and too many things can go wrong."

Vern Hoyt slanted a look at him. "I can't see that it's your worry. Didn't you tell me they just got themselves a new peace marshal—this fellow Gerringer? Keeping order's up to him."

"That's one thing that worries me," Murdock confessed. "I haven't quite got that man figured. If there's trouble, it's hard to say what way he'll jump, except that he's going to want to impress the people that hired him. Not knowing this outfit, he can make a bad mistake in judgment and the wrong ones can get hurt."

"Then what are you thinking?"

"I'm thinking we can't depend on the owners. Sherm Watkins isn't up to handling a situation, and Jed Finch is worse than nothing. So what about it, Vern?" he demanded. "I've got a feeling I might be needed in town tonight; can I leave you in charge here?"

Vern Hoyt rubbed his lantern jaw. "Do I get the bonus?" Before Murdock could answer he grinned briefly and punched the other lightly on the shoulder. "Sure, go ahead," he grunted. "I promise the herd'll be here when you get back."

CHAPTER V

For Eden Grove, it was a day of anticipation. Hearing at last that the Pool herd had actually been sighted, men left their places of business and went tramping out to stand in the high weeds of the riverbank, staring across as five thousand head of longhorn cattle poured off the low bluff and onto yonder flats. A late sun gilded the dusty fog kicked up by the herd. The hot plains wind brought a smell of dust and dung and far places, a rumble of hoofs and bawling of cows and squeal of horses, and the shouts of riders getting the big drive settled.

Though this was only one herd, they reasoned that there had to be others somewhere on the trail behind it; it was just a matter of time. Already mental cash registers were ringing up future profits.

Dust settled; shadows lengthened. Presently the trail-camp cookfire began to be answered by a glow of oil lamps in the raw wooden buildings along Railroad Avenue. Out of a slow summer dusk the first riders came splashing through the river shallows and into town. There were four of them. A shod hoof struck a single metallic chime as their horses leaped the tracks of the Santa Fe, then came to a milling halt while the riders looked the town over and made their choices.

The town in turn looked *them* over. Despite its brief existence Eden Grove had seen its share of hard men—gamblers, teamsters and track layers from the railroad gangs, troopers from Fort Larned, a buffalo hunter or two. But the reputation laid down in the other Kansas towns by Texans such as these, fresh off the long cattle trails, gave the new arrivals a special aura.

Phil Steadman said to the marshal, "Where would you bet they go first?"

The two men stood on the porch of the hotel, in the shadow of the veranda roof, a solid meal just eaten in the dining room. Gerringer held an unlighted cigar and a kitchen match he had dug from a pocket of his coat. As the pair considered the clot of horsemen, the lawman replied, "I'd say they'll pick the biggest and gaudiest saloon."

"That'll be Cotton's," the mayor said.

"Care to lay a bet?" Gerringer suggested, but the other shook his head.

"I'll take your word for it. Let's watch and see. . . ."

Out in the street, the riders ended their debate and with one accord kicked their horses forward. One took a gun from his holster and without warning let off a couple of shots skyward. The reports echoed off the false fronts of the buildings and caused one of the horses to shy, and its rider had to pull it down, cursing. One of his friends said loudly, "Oh, hell, Gater! Put that damn thing away." Another exclaimed, "Sure! You ain't even drunk yet!" The man they called Gater swore at them but didn't use the pistol again. There were hitchrails in front of some of the buildings lining the north side of Railroad Avenue, and the foursome put their animals to one of these, then dismounted and noisily trooped inside the brightly lit entrance of Lew

Cotton's saloon, letting the slatted door bang and swing behind them.

"Just as well I didn't bet," Phil Steadman commented dryly. "What about the shooting?"

"Too soon to make an issue," Gerringer said. "They'd only resent it. Better to wait until it genuinely looks as though it could get serious."

The mayor said, "I'm sure you know best." Jay Gerringer raked the match down the roof support and touched the spurting flame to the end of his cigar.

Sound of the gunshots carried, in early evening stillness, to a building a block away on Federal Street where that week's issue of the Eden Grove *Gazette* was being readied for the press. Clark Tanner glanced over at his pressman, Parley Newcome, and saw that the older man had looked up from the page form he was locking in. Grizzled head tilted to one side, ink-marked hands stilled in their work, Newcome listened, but there was no repetition of the sound against the chorus of crickets chirping in dry weeds outside the print shop's screened windows. Jimmy Lawless, the twelve-year-old who was Tanner's apprentice, came in from the back room dragging a bale of newsprint. The boy exclaimed, "Did you hear that?"

Parley Newcome answered, "Yeah, we heard. Sounds like Texas has arrived in Eden Grove." The old man looked over at his boss. "I suppose you'll be going down to count the bodies."

"No hurry." Tanner changed a word in the story he

had just written, got up from his desk and limped over to put it on the spike for Newcome to set. "No reason to think anyone has to get killed just because a trail crew has finally hit town. After all, I was told there's only thirty men in the outfit. It's a big one, but hardly what I'd call an invasion."

"Sho'!" the older man agreed scornfully. "We keep hearing about these tough Texans! I wonder how they'd stack up alongside the gandy-dancing Irish I used to see back in 'sixty-seven when I was following the building of the U.P. through Wyoming."

"I can imagine they're tough enough," Tanner said. "I'll be having a look for myself a little later."

Jimmy Lawless said hopefully, "When you do, can I come along? I never seen an honest-to-gosh cowboy close up!"

"Not tonight, Jimmy," Tanner told him. "Not with your folks out of town, and me promising to look after you. Railroad Avenue is no place for you right now.

"Come on, let's get this paper put to bed!"

In pairs and in small groups, more riders were coming into Eden Grove off the herd ground and across the shallow ford. The sound of their horses ran ahead of them, before they shaped up out of the darkness where lights gleamed on the railroad tracks, and on the single shining streak of telegraph wire looped on its poles along the right of way. Peter Duffy, his considerable bulk all but filling the doorway of his New York Restaurant, watched the nearly silent arrival and found something strange in it.

Before opening a place of his own, Duffy had worked in other restaurants, both as a pearl diver and a cook. He had seen Abilene at its peak as the center of the Texas trade, and he could well remember how the usual trail crew would hit town—at a rush and all together, wild young riders determined that everyone should know their particular outfit had arrived. Not these; they seemed to be avoiding one another, as though they came from hostile camps. He noticed that some joined the first noisy bunch who had taken over Cotton's big saloon, while others deliberately stayed away from there, choosing instead to rack their horses in front of the street's smaller places.

Very odd, Peter Duffy thought. He was a man who noticed such things, and puzzled over them.

Two riders, having caught sight of the letters painted on the restaurant's lighted window, reined before him. As Duffy straightened from his lean, one asked from the saddle, "This eat shack open for business?"

"Right you are," Duffy told him pleasantly. "Make yourselves to home." He stood aside as they swung down off their saddles, looped the reins over a tie pole, and went in. It was a small establishment, a couple of tables and a row of stools lined up against the counter. "I usually close earlier than this," Duffy told his customers, waddling around behind the counter as they took stools. "But I thought there might be somebody with an appetite for something beside trail-camp rations."

They were sun-darkened, their clothing worn, hair

76

hanging nearly to their shoulders. One thumbed his sweat-stained hat back from a startlingly white forehead and demanded in an unmistakable Texas drawl, "What's on the menu?"

"How does a steak strangled in onions sound to you? Or a mess of catfish, taken out of the river only this morning?"

"*Now* you're reading my mind!" The second puncher added, "What that belly robber we been eating after, all the way from Texas, can do to a pot of beans is scandalous."

Duffy shook up the fire in his stove and added a couple of lengths of cottonwood, the dance of the flames reflected on his hairless, gleaming skull. "You know, it's a funny thing," he commented as he got a fry pan. "But I'd understood all you boys in town tonight were from the same outfit. I'm beginning to think I maybe understood wrong—I mean, the way I see you split up and head for different saloons."

One of the cowboys gave a shrug. "We're all part of a pool. Us two is Sherm Watkins riders, but just because we had to trail all the way here with Tate Corman and his crowd, it sure as hell don't mean we have to drink with them, too!"

Duffy gave them a shrewd look. "So it's like that." Then the fish from the cooler was sizzling in the hot pan too noisily for talk.

"No charge, boys," Peter Duffy said later as he set the plates in front of his customers. "Special deal, this evening only. Your meal's on the house."

Somebody had got the mechanical piano at Cotton's to thumping, and its familiar racket poured out upon the evening, punctuated by male laughter and the squeals of the girls who worked in the saloon. But there was something new in Eden Grove tonight: a sound of big-roweled spurs scraping the dirt pathways, or ringing clear on the stretches of wooden sidewalk a few Railroad Avenue merchants had laid down before their places of business. No railroad section hand ever rang up a sound like that, nor did any sodbuster's heavy work shoes. The Texans made a stir out of all proportion to their actual numbers as they clomped the sidewalks and tramped in and out of the saloons and stores.

Sam Harolday was sweeping out the central aisle of the mercantile when a couple of men from the trail herd entered. Harolday looked them over with ill-concealed distaste. One was a hulk of a man, with massive shoulders and a battered face; the other had a whiskey bottle in each hand, and paused just inside the door to take swallows from them both, while his companion approached Harolday with the rolling stride of a man used to the saddle. Without preliminaries he demanded, "You got any eatin' tobacco?"

"I do indeed," the storekeeper answered coldly.

"So, gimme a couple of slabs."

Without a word Harolday put aside his broom and went around behind the counter. He was a man of great dignity, slim and distinguished in appearance, with a touch of gray at the temples that made him look rather

78

more like a successful banker than the operator of a mercantile in a raw frontier village. He got out two packages of chewing tobacco and laid them on the counter, then looked expectantly at his customer.

The Texan hesitated, scowling, and said roughly, "You ain't gonna make me *pay* for these, are you? Places along the street have been handing out free likker. Even the barber's shaving guys for nothing."

Harolday's stare, despite the size of the other man, never wavered. "Well," he replied, "*here* you pay."

The puncher's face darkened. As he hesitated, sizing up the unyielding man who confronted him, his friend over at the door took another drag on one of his bottles and said, "Aw, hell. Give him his money, Tate, and let's go. It's no fun here."

But Tate Corman had let his stare slide past Harolday to the curtained opening at the rear of the store, and at once his eyes widened and he showed his teeth in a grin. "Hey, now!" he grunted. "Pardner, you could just be wrong about *that!*"

Following his gaze, Harolday saw the handsome blond woman who had drawn aside the curtain and was looking out at them. At once the storekeeper felt his face stiffen. "Lucy!"

She frowned at Harolday's sharp tone, and at the angry motion of his head, but she quickly stepped back and the curtain dropped in place again. The damage had been done, however. Sam Harolday saw the raffish look the big puncher threw at him.

"Does that there belong to you?" Tate Corman demanded.

"She happens to be my wife."

"The hell!"

"You heard me," Harolday snapped. "And I don't need her being eyed by common trash off the streets!"

The big man's grin lost its humor, then changed to something ugly. His broad cheeks reddened. "You better look out who you're calling trash, mister—" The words broke off when he saw the hogleg revolver Harolday had brought out from under the counter, and was pointing at his face.

"I'll not waste words on you," Sam Harolday told him, his mouth trembling with fury. "Lew Cotton has girls who'll give you what you're looking for; don't come looking for it *here!* And you can pass the word to your friends: Any place my wife is, that's off limits— to all of you! Now pay for the tobacco and get out!"

Corman stared at him, and at the gun. There was a rubber-handled sixshooter in a holster rig strapped to the puncher's leg, but he made no reckless move to touch it. Over by the door the other Texan laughed and chided scornfully, "You better do what the man says, Tate, or he just might shoot you!"

The big man swung his shoulders as though to loosen them, and without looking around told his companion, "You shut the hell up!" He dug a silver dollar from his jeans and rang it on the counter. Gun unwavering, Sam Harolday reached into the cash box and made change. Corman snatched up the coins and his purchase, jerked about and went clomping out of there, spurs ringing defiantly.

As he passed his friend he caught the man with a

shoulder and staggered him. Then both were gone. Only then did Sam Harolday begin to shake.

He followed as far as the door, slammed it shut, and shoved the latch home. That done, Harolday drew a breath deep into his lungs. His face was grim as he returned the gun to the place where he kept it, beneath the counter, and stepped through the curtained doorway into the living quarters at the rear of the store.

The room had been meant for storage, and might one day be used for that purpose. As of now it was the only place in a raw and unfinished town that Sam Harolday had been able to find as housing for his family. What furnishings they possessed crowded the space that had to do them for living, eating, and sleeping, and even with the crude sliding windows fully opened, all the heat of a long August day seemed to be concentrated here. In the corner that served as a bedroom, Lucy Harolday was putting a little girl into her crib, a lovely blond miniature of herself. Harolday came over and stood angrily staring at his wife for a moment before he finally exploded.

"Did you have to do that? Show yourself to those men?"

Lucy straightened and turned on him, her face flushed. "*Show* myself!" she echoed indignantly. "I didn't even know you had customers. I only looked in to say that Jeanie wanted to kiss you good night, if you found the time. And what was wrong with that?"

He had no answer. They looked at each other in one of the hostile silences that so often fell between them. The ticking of a cheap clock on a shelf filled the moment, and there were other sounds that came in from the breathless night beyond the window—the battering of the ancient piano in Cotton's saloon, the sudden shrill whoop of a woman's laughter that was rather more like a scream.

Harolday gave a toss of his handsome head. "You heard *that,* I guess! I don't know if you realize it, but before the night is over things along this street could get very rough. I'll be just as pleased if none of those Texans know about you at all. About Jeanie either, for that matter."

She stared into his frowning face and said slowly, "I believe you're actually frightened for us! But . . . surely you knew what it would be like when you brought us to this town!"

It was an old quarrel between them, and Sam Harolday, his mouth gone hard, refused to be drawn again into the futile debate. Without answering, he strode past her to the rear door that led to the alley behind the store building. He looked into the darkness, closed the door, and snicked the sliding lock into place. He turned back to his wife. "Whatever happens, I don't want you opening that door tonight—not to anyone, not for any reason." Taking her silence to mean obedience, he left her and went into the store.

He was still trembling, partly in reaction to that scene with the Texans, partly in resentment of what he saw as Lucy's willful lack of understanding. He set to work putting covers on things, closing display cases, shutting down for the night, too engrossed with his mood to be wholly conscious of much that he was doing.

It had been a long time since Fortune had looked with favor on Sam Harolday, though he knew all too well that his wife didn't see these failures as bad luck, but as the fruits of his own poor business sense. Coming to this Godforsaken place to manage another man's store, for a pittance, had been only the latest sacrifice in the struggle to provide for his family. And now Virgil Beason, the cofounder of Eden Grove and the man who had hired him, was dead, and no one could even say for sure whom the store belonged to, or how much longer he would be able to keep this job.

Sam Harolday knew he had been a disappointment to his wife, but at a time like this a man deserved at least some sympathy, and not her continual coldness and faultfinding. He was so caught up in his bitter and self-pitying mood that it was some time afterward—and far too late—when he remembered he had forgotten to kiss his little girl good night.

CHAPTER VI

Ben Murdock moved through the darkness along Railroad Avenue, getting the feel of the night. So far things seemed to be going well enough. The two factions that made up the Pool crew appeared to have sorted themselves out, like oil and water that refused to mix. They were keeping strictly apart, and the friction that worried him hadn't developed into anything much as yet.

Liquor flowed freely. The moment he stuck his head in at the Kansas Bar, he was hailed by some of his friends and hauled up to the cheap plank counter where the bartender poured him a free drink he couldn't very well refuse. A little later he looked across the batwings at the crowd in Cotton's place but didn't enter, though he spotted Tate Corman and his friends among the sprinkling of townspeople, homesteaders, and railroad men.

This saloon was more garish and brightly lighted than the others. And it was noisier, with a mechanical piano and with gambling in progress, and there were women. Murdock spotted the man he took to be Lew Cotton himself, a stocky figure with a black mustache like a pirate's, who moved about the big room with the manner of an owner. He looked like someone able to keep things under control, and Murdock was satisfied to leave him Tate Corman and his cronies to handle.

That put him in mind of the one Eden Grove had hired just that day as its peace marshal, and by coincidence, as he turned from the entrance to Cotton's, he caught sight of Jay Gerringer moving away from him along the weed-grown pathway. Murdock regarded the spare, erect shape and the unmistakable set of the lawman's shoulders, visible in the lampglow from a nearby window. Then darkness swallowed him, a last unhurried echo of his footsteps reaching Murdock's ears as the marshal struck a stretch of wooden sidewalk. Patrolling his town, earning his pay . . . something in the thought sobered Murdock, and made him frown.

For Ben Murdock was a Texan who too often had seen what passed for "law" in some of these Kansas towns. As long as things were quiet, and the business owners remained satisfied, all well and good; but it was never more than a truce at best, and if something happened and matters got even briefly out of control, one was apt to see beatings, shootings, and pistolwhipping of unarmed trailhands by arrogant toughs who wore their authority pinned to their shirtfronts. Though Jay Gerringer seemed a cut above the usual run, Murdock could not predict what kind of adversary he might turn out to be if he thought his position in Eden Grove was threatened.

He shrugged, telling himself that everything seemed quiet and thinking, *If Gerringer thinks he's got the street under control, I for one am satisfied to turn it over to him!* Murdock had made himself certain promises, and now was as good a time as any to keep them.

He found the place he wanted, a newly finished

building next to Harolday's store. The arc of fancy lettering painted on the window identified it: "DRY GOODS & CLOTHING, Robert Truitt, Mgr." It was open, despite the hour, and oil lamps showed the racks of men's coats and suits, the cheap gingham dresses hanging from the ceiling, bins of shoes, shelves piled with bolts of cloth and with hats stacked one inside the other. As Murdock entered, a man came from the back of the store. He was a thin young man in shirtsleeves and waistcoat, a tape measure draped around his neck. He had bony features, a wild shock of black hair, quick and intelligent brown eyes. "You're with the trail herd," he said at once, noting the stranger's worn and grimy clothing.

"How did you guess?" Murdock commented dryly. "The boots are still serviceable. Otherwise I need everything new, from the skin out!"

"You bet!" The man indicated his stock with a wave of his bony hand. "Help yourself. Look around, see what I've got. Truitt's the name." After Murdock introduced himself, the other said, "If you find what you want, to a member of your outfit it's yours for fifty per cent off."

"That's generous enough," Murdock said. They discussed the trail, and the town, while he made his pick: two new shirts, pants, socks, underwear. He also looked over Truitt's selection of headgear, but this ran to derbies and broad-brimmed farmer's hats—nothing a Texas trail-herd drover could bring himself to wear; so he ended by retaining his battered Stetson, sweat-marked and nearly shapeless but still with a good many miles of hard use left in it.

The two young men chatted briefly, finding themselves oddly congenial despite the great difference in their backgrounds. Bob Truitt was from St. Louis. A small inheritance had allowed him to set up a business. He had not been in good health and had been advised that the high, dry Kansas plains might be good for him. He became a little envious as he measured himself against someone like Ben Murdock, with his vigorous life and free existence as a cattle drover. Presently Murdock paid his bill, exchanged "good evenings," gathered up his purchases, and carried them outside, where he met Phil Steadman and John Riggs, just passing.

The doctor eyed the bundles. "It appears you've been shopping."

"Correct. The next step is to throw away everything I've got on," Murdock told them. "But first I want a bath, so I can stand myself again! I was wondering if I can get one at the barber's."

"Joe Mullens ain't equipped," Steadman said. "Besides, with the customers he's got lined up waiting, it'd take you an hour even to get a shave. No, you come to the hotel, friend. I'll give you a room, and see that a tub's brought up and plenty of hot water."

Murdock hesitated. "That sounds just fine—only, I'm not staying in town tonight. I've got to be getting back out to the herd."

"Suit yourself. But you're going to be around a few days, and you'll be wanting a headquarters. Take the room, and use it as you need to. There'll be no charge."

Ben Murdock shook his head a little at the generosity

of the offer. "I must say, this town is certainly doing its best to make this outfit feel welcome. I've never seen the likes of it, any other town I've been."

"We've got our reasons," John Riggs answered seriously. "It's a special night for Eden Grove. No matter how many more herds of Texas beef go through those shipping pens, there'll never again be a *first* one."

"I'll be glad to take you up on the room," Murdock told the hotelman, "and I thank you for it." He turned to Doc Riggs. "What news do you have for me about Wally McKay?"

"Your man's resting peacefully," the doctor assured him. "I expect the fever to break by morning. My office is over on Federal. Feel free to drop in and see him anytime."

"Thanks," Murdock said, and meant it.

He left the two councilmen to their tour of the town, and went back to where he had his horse tied. The livery barn, with an oil lantern burning above the entrance, was the last building at the western end of the street. Murdock rode in and stepped down, giving the reins of the bay to the night hostler who commented, "Looks like a good horse."

"He is, and he's trailed a lot of miles 'twixt here and Texas. A long time since he's enjoyed a good rubdown and a clean stall," he told the man. "And let him have some oats—he's earned them. I'll be around for him later."

"Right!"

Tom McDougall had built large, evidently looking toward a booming business sometime in the future, but tonight the stalls were mostly vacant and sounds chased their echoes through the big barn's empty spaces. As Murdock tossed the other a silver cartwheel and turned to leave, carrying his bundles and his saddlebags, a door suddenly wrenched open and someone came charging out of a cubicle adjoining the closed-off tack room. It was McDougall himself. On a desk, in the little room he had left, a ledger lay open in a circle of lamplight, indicating that he had been sitting there working over his accounts. From the cast of his gaunt face he seemed to be on the lookout for trouble; perhaps the sound of voices had alarmed him. His scowl rested on Murdock for a moment, and on the hostler and the bay. Next instant his head whipped about as a hoof struck a timber somewhere back in the barn's shadowed stall area.

Guessing the cause of the man's behavior, knowing it probably had to do with a trail outfit in town, Murdock wasn't sure whether to be amused or angry. But he said pleasantly, "Good evening."

Tom McDougall looked at him. "What?" he grunted. Then, feeling called on to explain, he added grumpily, "I heard something going on, couldn't tell what it might be." He gave his hostler a meaningful look and a jerk of the head that caused the man at once to lead Murdock's horse away into the depths of the building, its iron shoes thudding hollowly in the stillness. The livery owner turned to the wide street doors, walked out onto the ramp, and stood with hands thrust into the hip pockets of his overalls, studying the night.

Murdock joined him, and together they surveyed

the street, listened to the jangle of the mechanical piano at Cotton's, and noted the lighted windows of the nearby hotel and the single spot of lantern burning in the two-by-four railroad depot beyond the steel tracks. "Warm night," Murdock said, and when that drew no answer he added, "You could use some rain here."

Tom McDougall admitted, "It's been a dry month."

"The country looks like it. Though we run into a pretty good storm a couple of nights ago," the Texan volunteered. "South on the trail . . ."

Suddenly the livery owner's head jerked around. The lantern overhead made hollows in his cheeks, and his eyes peered narrowly at the other man. "Murdock!" he snapped. "Why waste our breath with small talk? So far things have been quiet enough, but I got a bad feeling about that outfit of yours. I've been up and down the street, listening to their talk, and I've heard enough to tell me there's something very wrong going on—bad feelings that could bust out in real trouble before the town is rid of them. But if any damage is done, you better know that I for one will be holding you personally responsible!"

"Why me? It's not my outfit," Murdock told him. "I got them to market, but there my authority ends. As for keeping the peace, the town council's hired a man to do that."

"Hired over my objections," the liveryman retorted, clipping the words short. "As I think you know! I ain't satisfied with that Gerringer. If I had my way we'd be shut of him."

"Meaning," the other said dryly, "you judge and reject a man before he's had a chance to perform. I wouldn't want *my* job depending on you!" He didn't wait for a reply. He said, "Good night," and walked away carrying his belongings, leaving McDougall scowling and digging at the short-cropped whiskers that fringed his lower jaw.

On the lot next to the hotel, Joe Mullens had his barber's layout, complete with everything except a building. A canvas stretched on poles protected the chair and the packing-case cabinet that held his tonics and soap and brushes and other equipment. Working by lantern-light, Mullens had a member of the Pool outfit stretched out in the chair with lather on his face. A half dozen others stood about as though awaiting their turns, but something caused Murdock to halt for a close second look.

It was the barber who gave him the warning. Mullens, a spidery little man with a saddle of thinning black hair combed carefully across his scalp, had paused in his work and stood as though frozen, the razor forgotten in his hand. As he watched the tableau, suddenly Murdock could see fear in him. No angry words were being spoken, but he saw now that attention was centered on one of Sherm Watkins' riders, a man named Harry Griffith, who stood facing Bart Haymes of the Wilson Stiles crew. Not knowing what he was interrupting, sensing only that something was about to erupt, Ben Murdock sharply called out Griffith's name. He had to repeat it before the puncher turned and looked at him with eyes that seemed blinded by some hot emotion.

"Over here, Harry," Murdock said, beckoning. "Something I want to ask you . . ."

For a moment he didn't know what result he would get, but Griffith was used to taking orders from Ben Murdock. Angrily reluctant, he came untracked from where he stood and stalked over to join the trail boss as the rest watched him go. Without waiting, Murdock turned and went on along the path, still carrying his saddlebags over one shoulder and his bundle of clothing under the other arm, and giving Harry Griffith no choice but to follow.

Only when they had reached the hotel, and a jutting corner of it shut off view of the improvised barber shop, did Murdock turn to face the puncher. "All right," he said sharply. "What was going on back there?"

Griffith had a short temper. His broad face colored and he exclaimed, "You said you had something to ask me. . . ."

"I sure as hell did, and that was it!" Murdock snapped. "You and Haymes were squared off, ready to tear into each other, with the rest of them just waiting for it. So you'd better start explaining!"

The other became uncomfortable under the questioning. He dropped his eyes. "Oh, you know, Ben. It was just one of those things. Somebody had a bottle they was passing—but damned if I drink with any outfit that lets a tinhorn like Pollard stay on the payroll!"

Murdock stared at him. "I suppose you told them that."

"Damn right I told them!"

The trail boss shook his head. He knew that Griffith had been a heavy loser to Dab Pollard's stacked deck, and he could understand the puncher's feelings. Even so, this was more than he could allow. He said sternly, "It was a dumb way to act, Harry! Were you trying to start a war? Now, when at last we've actually got the drive behind us?"

"If *they* want one," the puncher retorted belligerently, "what better time than now? And who's gonna bother to stop it?"

"Me, for onc! I fought hard, holding this outfit together; I won't stand by and see it fall apart! I want you to stay entirely away from that Stiles bunch. I ask it as a favor. Long as we're in town, we've got to do what we can to hold trouble to a minimum. How about it—will you help me?"

The puncher seemed to consider it. He screwed up his face as he turned to look toward the barber shop. He pulled off his hat and ran a hand across his yellow hair, which hung shaggily over his ears and almost to the collar of his shirt. "Oh, well," he said finally. "I've went this long without a haircut; I can go a little longer."

"Thanks," Murdock said. "I appreciate this. . . ." He watched Harry Griffith move on along the street, and then climbed the hotel's steps and entered the lobby.

Phil Steadman had been there ahead of him and left orders concerning him at the desk. The room Murdock was taken to by the hotel owner's redheaded nephew was up the uncarpeted stairs and at the front of the building, overlooking Railroad Avenue. The hotel being new, the room was free of the trapped odors of dust and stale cooking and too many previous occupants typical of other hotels where Ben Murdock had stayed. It was small but adequately furnished, with an iron bedstead that hadn't started sagging yet, a commode, a straight-backed chair and a wardrobe in one corner. Murdock deposited his belongings on floor and chair and went to open the window, letting in the warm breath of the night.

He checked his appearance in the mirror over the wash stand, and shuddered a little. A man on a trail drive, with nothing to remind him, was apt to overlook the result of going for weeks without a decent shave. It sent him to his saddlebags to get out his razor with the yellowing ivory handle. He stripped off his sweaty shirt and tossed it in a corner, and was pouring cold water into the hand basin when a knock came at the door. Barney Osgood entered carrying a tin tub, followed by a black woman who had two steaming pails of water from the kitchen. The young redhead explained, "Uncle Phil said you put in orders for a bath. . . ."

Murdock shook his head. "I was only wishing," he said. "It would be nice if I had time to spare on such luxuries! Leave it, though," he added quickly. "I can enjoy a shave, at least—with hot water!" It was a real pleasure, when they were gone, to work up a lather and let it soak into his wiry beard, and then run the razor through it with clean, sweeping strokes. But then there was the rest of the water going to waste, getting cold, and the fresh new clothes, never worn, waiting to be put on.

Below his window the street lay silent and things seemed to be peaceful enough. The temptation was too great. Murdock filled the tub and stretched out, determined to make the most of it, but a guilty conscience interfered with the leisurely soaking he had long been promising himself. He did a hurried job, finished by scrubbing the dirt and sweat from his hair, and long before he was willing climbed out and reached for a towel. Even so, he felt considerably better—like a new man, almost, as he got into the clothes he'd bought at Truitt's. He rubbed up his boots a little, used a comb and strapped his gunbelt in place. Then, reasonably satisfied, he blew out the lamp and stepped into the hallway.

The long corridor, splitting the hotel's second story and lined with numbered doorways, was poorly lighted by a couple of wall lamps. He surprised a pair who stood near the head of the stairs leading to the lobby. As Murdock approached the man turned slightly and he glimpsed Jed Finch's lantern-jawed face, framed by wings of lank, mouse-colored hair. Finch had the woman crowded back against the stairwell's railing, one rope-scarred hand resting on the newel post in a way that held her pinned. He was saying in his loud and rasping voice, "I know you ain't going to be busy *all* night. Now you just tell me what time you figure to be getting off."

By now Murdock had a better view of the woman,

and he saw that she was no more than a girl. She looked frightened. She had drawn back against the railing, as far away from the man as she could get, and had an armload of towels and pillowcases that she clutched tightly and used as a shield. Murdock heard her say, a little breathlessly, "No . . . please!"

Jed Finch wasn't one to be put off. He continued, as loudly as before, "Honey, maybe you think I'm only stringin' you. Hell, I ain't one of them dumb cowpokes who's gone through his pay already. Not me! I'm one of the *owners* of this herd. Down in Texas, anyone'll tell you Jed Finch is an important man. Here—take a look at this." He dug into his jeans and fetched out a wad of bills and silver. "Believe me, honey, it'll pay you to be nice to me this evening!"

The girl could only shake her head. She was a little thing, with a lot of dark hair done up on her head to keep it out of her way. Ben Murdock judged her to be a hotel maid in the employ of Phil Steadman, and probably new at it; at least she plainly didn't know how to deal with somebody like Jed Finch. She looked pale in the wan glow of the lamp in its wall bracket. Trapped, she glanced anxiously about, and that was when she saw Murdock approaching.

He had seen more than enough. Anger and disgust were in his voice as he said harshly, "Let her alone, Jed. Get away from her!"

Finch hadn't been aware of his presence. He jerked about, and when he saw the trail boss he stiffened with surprise and quick anger. "Murdock! Who asked you to horn in?"

"Nobody, I guess. But you're making a nuisance of yourself. Even you ought to see she doesn't want anything to do with you."

"Why, damn you!" The man's craggy fists drew up hard, and for a moment Murdock thoroughly expected the Pool rancher to take a swing at him. He stood his ground and the fist Finch had half raised was slowly lowered. Murdock looked past him at the girl, and gave her a brief nod. She had stood transfixed, watching them both with wide and startled eyes, but she got his message. For the moment free of Jed Finch's attention, she hastily turned and fled while she could.

Left alone with the rancher, Murdock told him bluntly, "I reckon you know there are women at Cotton's saloon down the street who'll sell you what you're looking for, so why don't you go find them? This girl . . ." His mouth hardened with contempt. "Jed, you've got a daughter at home that's not much younger than she is! In your place, I'd say about now I'd have to feel a little ashamed of myself!"

"By damn, I won't be lectured by *you!*" Jed Finch roared in a voice that boomed through the hallway. Murdock must have stung him, for all at once his face was flushed with something more than the booze that soured his breath. Suddenly he missed the girl, and looked around, hunting for her in vain. He let go with an obscenity. Murdock merely continued to regard him coldly. Seeing no good reason to go on with this, Finch gave an angry shrug of his high, narrow shoulders and abruptly swung away, brushing past the trail boss as he made for the head of the stairs.

He paused only long enough to tilt back his head and hurl a last warning across the banister railing: "Don't get the idea this is over with. You'll hear from me later!" The other made no reply, and Finch went clomping down the uncarpeted stairway. Ben Murdock, watching him go, was quite sure the Pool owner could be counted on to mean just what he said.

Murdock turned to look for the girl. After withdrawing from the argument she had watched discreetly at a little distance, with her shoulders pressed against a closed door and still hugging her armload of linen. Approaching, Murdock could see she was trembling. He could see, too, that she had a very neat and attractive figure which the plain shirtwaist and drab skirt couldn't disguise, and despite the pallor of anxiety her face, with its enormous dark eyes and delicately molded features, was decidedly attractive. She *was* young, he saw now—perhaps no more than seventeen—but her figure was that of a woman.

He said quickly, "He didn't hurt you?"

"No—no," she insisted, shaking her head. "But he sure had me scared!" She hesitated, then blurted out, "Honest, I never said or did anything that woulda let him think . . ."

"I never supposed you did," he told her gently, when she couldn't bring herself to finish the statement. Trying to put her at ease, he said, "You work here, do you? At the hotel?"

The girl nodded. Raising a hand that still shook a little, she pushed back the heavy mass of hair from her forehead. "My folks are homesteaders," she explained.

"There's never enough cash money, and so when I had the chance at this job, it seemed a way I could help out—though they really didn't want me to do it. I know they were afraid I might run into situations like—like that one."

"It's altogether too easy, sometimes," Murdock agreed. "Though I hope you won't judge all Texans by Jed Finch!"

She hesitated, then said, "You know him. . . . Do you suppose he could be the kind to make trouble for me with Mr. Steadman, all because I—because I wouldn't—?"

"He'd damn well better not! What's your name?"

"Amy. Amy Grover."

"I'll have a talk with Steadman, Amy," he promised. "Just in case. I'll explain exactly what happened. Oh, one more thing: I'm Ben Murdock. I'm the trail boss of the outfit that's here in town, and I sort of feel responsible. I'd like you to promise: If any of my people give you further trouble, you're to let me know. Will you do that?"

She searched his face, and then a hint of a smile softened the anxiety in her own. "Sure," she said. "I promise. That's real thoughtful. Thanks, Mr. Murdock."

He returned the smile, and left her.

CHAPTER VII

The office of the Eden Grove *Gazette* was empty at the moment except for the printer, Parley Newcome, who had his hands full with the ancient hand press and with the run of tomorrow morning's paper. The temperamental old press seldom got through a job of any size without something going wrong, and this time it had thrown a bolt. Newcome was down on hands and knees, swearing as he hunted for it on the splintered floorboards, when the door opened. Irritably he reared back on his haunches and squinted at the man who entered, failing to recognize him. "Yeah?" he said gruffly. "If you're looking for the boss, you've just missed him. Tanner stepped out, not five minutes ago."

Without speaking, the man came out of the shadows and into the light of the lamp, and Newcome had a better look at him—the spare figure, the somber cast of the man's features. A shiny bit of metal pinned to the stranger's coat identified him. Parley Newcome reached up, caught the edge of his work bench and hoisted himself to his feet. "From the badge, you'd have to be Jay Gerringer," he said. "Well, I can tell you—after the story I was given to set up about you, I been just a mite curious to see what a sure-enough mankiller looks like."

Gerringer had halted and was looking around at the layout of the shop—the press and the compartmented type boxes, Newcome's work table and the editor's desk, the overflowing cabinets and the general orderly confusion. "And you're the printer," he said. "I believe Tanner said your name was Newcome."

"Always has been."

The flippant manner of his speech got him a sharp look, as though the other man sensed that he was making no effort to hide his disapproval. Instead of answering, however, Gerringer indicated the pile of freshly printed sheets on the work table. "Tomorrow's paper?"

Newcome nodded, but when Gerringer reached for one the old man informed him sharply, "That'll cost you a nickel." With a shrug the marshal dug out a coin and dropped it on the table before helping himself to one of the flat, glistening, still-wet sheets. Watching him, the printer wiped his hands on a bit of waste and then picked up a cold meat sandwich from the work table and began to munch on it.

Gerringer, as though finding nothing to interest him, passed over the lead story, which dealt with the arrival of the first herd of Texas beef at Eden Grove. Instead his eyes moved down the page until he found what he was looking for. Parley Newcome could guess what it was. Never one who hesitated to say anything that crossed his mind, he observed dryly, "The way you eat up that story about yourself, a body would think this was Kansas City and it was the *Journal of Commerce* or some other big paper—not just a four-page weekly in a town nobody's ever likely to hear of."

Jay Gerringer lifted his head, rested his eyes on the older man, and said in a voice without emotion,

"You're pretty hostile toward me, apparently."

Unabashed, Newcome told him, "I just don't think I care for your type. You remind me of some I used to see, that followed the U.P. construction camps. Peace officers, they liked to call themselves. Hell, they didn't care nothing about law and order! For a price, they'd use their guns anytime to keep the work crews from getting out of line. And if they had to kill a few now and then, it didn't matter to them or to the bosses that hired 'em."

"So you rate me with that sort?"

Parley Newcome stuffed the last of the sandwich in his mouth. "We'll all have to wait and see, won't we? Rumor has it you got the name of a bad risk after what went on up there in Leavenworth. If you want to hold *this* job there's one man in particular you damn well got to please. Reckon we both know what I'm talking about."

Jay Gerringer said coldly, "Suppose you spell it out. . . ."

Newcome didn't mind. "I mean Tom McDougall, of course. Most of us in Eden Grove are happy to see those Texans, but Tom's going to want a tight lid kept, even if it means using your gun on a few of them.

"Well, I've known some Texans. Try to run them McDougall's way and you just might cause more grief than the town can handle. Contrariwise, you go *too* easy and Tom may have your badge." The printer wagged his head knowingly. "I ain't sure I'd want to be standing in your boots, Gerringer. But somehow I'm willing to bet it'll be an interesting show!"

102

For a long moment the eyes in that enigmatic face regarded him. Then, deliberately, Jay Gerringer folded the paper he had purchased and thrust it into a pocket of his coat. "You think of *everything* as a show, don't you?" he said as he turned to leave. "For your personal entertainment. Well, I trust you'll enjoy this one."

He didn't wait for an answer.

The crowd in Brady's Bar was beginning to loosen up and grow noisier as the drinks the trail crew had been taking on started to have their effect. With the sharp edge of a deep-scated thirst blunted, and with the rest of the evening ahead of them, argument arose as to how they wanted to spend it. A number were trying without much satisfaction to pump the owner of the place for information about the women available in town. Nick Brady wasn't eager to lose his trade, either to the talent at Cotton's or to another set of females who had established themselves in a pair of surplus Army tents at the western edge of the townsite, to service the railroad men and other transients.

A half dozen Texans, finding themselves once more with money in their pockets, were making their own diversion: They had gotten cards at the bar and had a game going at one of the tables, their tobacco smoke hanging in the air in layers and hand-rolled cigarette butts beginning to litter the floor around their boots. When presently a new arrival came into the saloon fairly bursting with excitement, it was to these poker players that he broke his news.

"Penny ante stuff!" he declared loudly. "You should see what *I* seen just now when I looked in at Cotton's. Would you believe it—Pollard's being took to the cleaner's!"

"You're funnin'!" Harry Griffith, himself an inveterate and unlucky gambler, pawed at the tawny mop of hair that still needed the cutting he had failed to get at the barber shop. He stared at the puncher. He had lost more than anyone else across the blanket on which the tinhorn had dealt his stacked decks. "Are you telling us somebody's actually getting to Dab Pollard?"

"You don't believe me, go have a look, but you better hurry! He's run up against a bigger crook than *he* is, a real pro from the look of him, a sharper with an eye that can slice you in two. I heard a name: Kilburn? Something like that. . . ."

Brady, behind the bar, knew the man. "That'd be Kimbrough," he said. "Full name, Mark Kimbrough. He's been around town a week or so, keeping to himself. Rumor says he left Wichita in kind of a hurry. Rumor says, too, he keeps a couple of pepperboxes in specially built pockets of his waistcoat."

"Well, whoever he is he's more than Pollard can handle. The way the game is going, I doubt our boy can last more than another couple hands."

"By God, this I got to see!" Harry Griffith had already tossed aside the deck he was dealing and was scooping his money off the table. He led the pack as these men of the Pool crew abandoned their game and their drinks and headed for the street, eager to watch the tables being turned on one they all bitterly disliked.

They left the batwings fanning vacant air behind them.

The tacit truce that had divided up the town between the factions was suddenly forgotten; Harry Griffith and his friends went tramping boldly into Cotton's. There, amid the din of the mechanical piano and the loud man-talk punctuated by an occasional piercing squeal from one or another of Lew Cotton's girls, they found Tate Corman, the Finch brothers, and a tight knot of Wilson Stiles riders. The newcomers were interested in only one thing, and went directly to a corner table where, in the weak glow of a bracketed oil lamp, the poker game was in progress.

Five players were sitting in: Jed Finch and a couple of locals, along with Dab Pollard and the man named Kimbrough who was supposedly putting him through the wringer. Things appeared to have arrived at a critical moment, judging by the looks on the faces of the players and the ring of spectators who had gathered to watch. Tate Corman was among these. He had his arm draped over the shoulders of one of the girls, but when he saw the newcomers approaching he quickly dropped the arm and his expression toughened.

Harry Griffith gave him no more than a glance; he was eyeing the sweat he could see glistening on Dab Pollard's flushed cheeks. Gone was all of the arrogance that had made him so obnoxious when he was winning. Pollard was hurting. As for the one who had brought him down, it was clear that this Mark Kimbrough had been described accurately enough; a professional gambler has a certain style that is hard to mistake. Kimbrough had the unhealthy complexion of one who spent too many late hours in smoky rooms. He also had agile fingers trained to handle cards and dice, and a steady stare that now rested on Dab Pollard's face as though it were a page in a book. Harry Griffith looked at the man's slim figure and well-cut clothing, and wondered about the pepperbox pistols in the waistcoat pockets.

Kimbrough said, "You're holding up the game, Pollard. I met your raise and I've raised you again. It will take the rest of what you have there in front of you to see what I'm holding."

Just then the mechanical piano quit and in the sudden quiet Dab Pollard's hoarse breathing became audible. He said in a strangled whisper, "Sonofabitch! You'd like to freeze me out, wouldn't you?"

Harry Griffith couldn't restrain himself from asking loudly, "How do you like it, Pollard—being on the other end for a change?"

The man lifted his head, as though aware for the first time of his enemies ringing the table. Others he had cheated began to add their taunts to Harry's. Someone declared, "He ain't got the guts to call!"

An angry bellow from Tate Corman overrode them. "Quit riding him, damn you! Let him make his play!" The voices quickly fell silent. But Dab Pollard had felt their sting; his face had reddened still more and the muscles of his clenched jaw bulged.

The game continued to wait while he had another look at the cards bunched in his fist. He still liked them, apparently. With every eye resting on him, he drew a long breath and proceeded to shove all that was left of his money to the center of the table. He told Kimbrough in a hoarse voice, "All right, damn you, I say I got you beat!"

"You do?" Deliberately the gambler laid out his hand. "Can you beat five hearts, the queen on top?"

Pollard stared in disbelief. He looked again at his own cards, and with a sudden furious gesture flung them away, face down. When they saw that, the men who had been hoping for his downfall let go in an eruption of catcalls and shouting laughter; they whooped and stomped and clapped one another on the shoulder. "Cleaned him out, by God!" someone crowed, while Mark Kimbrough, without any expression at all, began to rake in the pot his heart flush had won.

Goaded past endurance, Pollard was on his feet, the chair crashing to the floor behind him. His empty hands were clenched as he told the one who had beaten him, "Damn it! You got to give me a chance to win this back!"

"If you think you can, I'm willing," the gambler said calmly. "Any time you're able to raise another stake."

"Where would he ever get it?" Harry Griffith demanded. "One thing sure: Nobody he's suckered before is gonna let him do it to 'em again! Hell, he's a picked chicken!"

Dab Pollard glared at the grinning faces. He started to yell something back at them, but instead only swung his head like a badgered bull. The next moment he turned away and in hot anger pushed through the ring of men around the table. Looking neither right nor left he plowed his way clear and went storming out of Cotton's, into the sweltering August night.

Ben Murdock, just passing, had to take a hurried step backward to avoid a collision. Pollard didn't seem to notice him. Murdock halted and watched the man rush past him, those big Mexican spurs chiming, to the horses at the saloon hitching rack. Pollard went directly to his own animal, a roan, and vaulted into the saddle. A haul at the bit sent the animal lunging back out of the lineup, and then Pollard yanked its head around and sank the spurs. The horse leaped under him and took off toward the moonlit river flats. In moments he was across the tracks and gone.

Staring after him, Murdock wondered what could have sent him charging out of the saloon and out of town like a man driven by his furies. It was even more disturbing, a moment later, to push through the swinging doors and there be confronted, amid the locals and townspeople, by both factions of his trail crew, which until then had been keeping strictly separated.

He heard angry voices at a table in a corner of the room, where all attention seemed to be focused. Quickly making his way over there, Murdock came up on one of his men and, taking him by an elbow, demanded sharply, "What's happening?"

The puncher was exultant. "You missed the fun. Dab Pollard just went and lost his roll—to someone who knows cards better'n him. Man named Kimbrough . . ."

Ben Murdock felt like swearing. Something told him this could be the very kind of trouble he had been trying to avoid. He had already recognized Tate Corman's voice, roughened by anger and the alcohol he had been drinking. Now, as he worked his way to the table, the trail boss could hear Corman castigating the one who had wiped out his friend Pollard, calling him a cheat and a tinhorn and every other vile name, seemingly intent on provoking the man—and himself, too—into a mood to fight. The bystanders had already drawn back, clearing a space about the table, and the rest of the players had left their chairs to get out of range, leaving only one man—the gambler—still seated there.

Face expressionless as though he didn't even know Tate Corman's diatribe was aimed at him, Kimbrough was quite methodically gathering his winnings, stacking silver coins and shaping the tumble of greenbacks into a single neat pile. Being ignored riled the big Texan even further. Murdock saw his shoulders move and settle, saw him move back a step and let his head drop forward and his right hand pull back. He seemed to have whipped himself up to the point of using the gun in his scuffed leather holster.

It didn't happen. One moment Kimbrough's swift hands were busy with his winnings; in the next breath one of those hands was holding a short-snouted derringer pistol trained on Corman's chest. The gambler said, with a voice like the cutting edge of a knife, "Lay off!"

At once there was a dead stillness. Tate Corman's thick chest swelled but no sound came out of him as he stared at the black bore of the weapon. The crowd, too, held its breath, and across the room a bartender laid down a whiskey glass and towel and unobtrusively edged over to the closed door of what was probably

Lew Cotton's private office. Murdock, watching, saw him knock, then turn the knob and slip inside. The door closed.

Mark Kimbrough, onehanded, was picking up his money and stowing it away in his clothing while the hideout gun kept its unrelenting threat aimed at Tate Corman's chest. The job finished, the gambler got to his feet and pushed the chair away with his heel. With the derringer between them he said icily to Corman, "Let me tell you something about me. I'm a pro; this is how I make my living. When I play against amateurs, I don't need any more edge than that. But your friend tried to cheat me—and it was the clumsiest try I ever saw! I simply gave him a lesson he had coming.

"As I said before, let him get hold of a stake and he's welcome to another chance at me. Tell him to play honest and so will I; you have my promise. But right now I'm walking out of here—and if you touch that gun I'll kill you! That's also a promise. . . ."

The bartender was back, having fetched his boss to show him what was going on. The practiced eye of the saloon owner sized up the situation at a glance, but though he scowled Lew Cotton held off, while the room waited. In a moment the big Texan made up his mind about the ultimatum he'd been given: Tate Corman brought his hands up and put them on the back of the chair Dab Pollard had vacated, and as he gripped the wood his white knuckles revealed the intensity of his feelings.

Kimbrough, for his part, seemed pleased to accept the truce. He nodded, and the derringer vanished as quickly as it had appeared. The gambler deliberately adjusted the hang of his coat and set his bowler straight. Then, in no particular hurry, he slipped between a couple of the bystanders and was on his way to the door.

With a great shout Tate Corman flung the chair away and started after him, skirting the table and scattering a couple of men standing in his way with a single sweep of his thick arm. His charge brought him face to face with Ben Murdock.

When he saw who was blocking his path, his head jerked up and he exclaimed, "Murdock, don't get in my way!"

The trail boss stood his ground and said flatly, "Cool off, Tate. The man's gone. Let him go!"

"Didn't you see? The sonofabitch pulled a hideout on me!"

"I saw—and if you corner him, he'll use it! This business ain't worth ruining our first night in town with a shooting. What does it matter if one tinhorn out-slicked another?"

The big man glared at him. "Damn you, Dab Pollard's my friend."

"Who got no more than he deserved. If he thinks he has a score with this fellow Kimbrough, then let *him* do the settling. Come on over to the bar, Tate—have a drink and forget it!"

"Drink with *you,* Murdock?" Tate Corman's face distorted in a look of pure malevolence. "Why, I'll see you in hell first!" He turned away, and a loud squeal of bootleather broke the silence.

Left standing there, and fighting back the quick swell of anger, Ben Murdock noted the waiting looks laid upon him by the men of his crew, and the curious stares of others in the big room. Suddenly he understood he could not walk away from this. At the trail camps he had been able to ignore the hatred and the insults of Tate Corman, because his crew understood the greater importance of the job he had been given. But now Corman had thrown his challenge at him in front of strangers, and if Murdock wanted to keep the respect of his men he could not let it pass. This time, he had no choice but to answer.

Corman had gone to the bar and propped his elbows on it, massive shoulders hunched, as he waited for the bartender to pour the drink he had signaled for. Murdock followed him over, deliberately ignoring the suspicious look he got from Lew Cotton, who was still watching as though with some foreknowledge of what was to come. Corman stood alone at the bar. Murdock halted a little distance away, put the point of an elbow on the wood, and said coldly, "All right, Tate. Just what is it going to take to satisfy you?"

Corman's head swiveled; his stare skewered the other man's, baleful and truculent. "You really asking?" he demanded in a bellowing voice that echoed throughout the listening quiet of the place. He straightened, taking his elbows off the bar. "You ready to shuck that gun and step outside into the street with me?"

"You want to settle this with a fight. . . ." Murdock looked at the huge fists, the rockhard knuckles that according to rumor could break a man's jaw in the kind of rough-and-tumble that was Tate Corman's specialty. It was not the first time he had measured himself against Tate Corman. Tate was big and tough and an experienced brawler, but one who relied on bull strength rather than intelligence. Though it would be a grueling experience, Murdock thought there was a fair chance he could take him if he had to. He was loath to try. He could feel the keen expectation in the room, but he shook his head. "Sorry. I can't oblige you."

Tate Corman let a sneer lift his upper lip. He threw a look past Murdock, at the listening crowd. "That don't surprise me. I always had you figured for a yellow-belly!"

Murdock refused to let himself be baited. "Oh no, Tate. Just happens I believe it's no way to settle any-thing. Yellow? I'd save *that* word for the man who'd draw a gun when his enemy's back was turned!"

As he had intended, that comment was lost on those who overheard it, but there was no chance Tate Corman wouldn't know what he was talking about—a day back along the trail, when Corman and Dab Pollard drove Murdock into the streambank cottonwoods with bul-lets, only to have him turn the tables and take their guns away from them. Narrowly watching the big man, Murdock saw Corman's face turn suddenly crimson with guilty anger. And he left him with it.

He had taken barely a step toward the street door when a sudden shout turned him. The warning was too late. Murdock had only a glimpse of Tate Corman, closing in. Then the big man was on top of him.

CHAPTER VIII

A fist struck a massive blow against the hinge of his jaw, and he was hurled aside by the force of it. Murdock would have gone down had he not staggered full tilt into a handful of spectators. They yelled in alarm and scattered out of the way, but the impact kept him on his feet. Hands grabbed and steadied him. Ben Murdock pulled loose and saw Corman descending on him, livid with rage, blind to everything but the urge to do damage. Yonder, Lew Cotton was gesturing angrily and shouting for the fight to be taken outside, but there was no way Murdock could oblige even if he had wanted to, for now Corman was aiming another blow at his skull.

Angry enough himself, his head ringing like a bell, Murdock threw up an arm and managed to knock the blow aside. It left Tate Corman unguarded and the trail boss swung a fist at what would have to be his most vulnerable point—the thick middle, just above a belt buckle made of hammered Mexican silver. The fist sank deep. Stopped in his tracks, Corman let the wind erupt through parted lips in a grunt of surprise and pain. Murdock took the opportunity to hit him in the chest and again in the belly, but then, as he tried to step clear, he felt powerful arms suddenly clamp around him.

He couldn't let himself be trapped in a bear hug that would easily crush his ribs. Desperate, Murdock quickly straightened and the top of his head caught his bigger opponent in the face. The arms fell away and

Corman stumbled back.

Murdock had lost his hat. He shook the hair out of his sweating face, dimly aware of pandemonium among the Pool riders, who had been split by weeks of growing enmity on the trail. Now even the bystanders to whom the brawl meant nothing were caught up in the excitement and were shouting at the fighters, yelling for a kill. Ben Murdock was alarmed but he could spare no thought to what was going on around him.

He wondered if Tate Corman remembered he had a gun in his holster. If so the big man showed no inclination to use it. He came lunging at his enemy instead, hands reaching to grab. Murdock, quicker than Corman, ducked out of his road and at the last moment lashed out and caught the other on the side of the head. There was sharp pain; as he circled free he shook his fingers, hoping he hadn't damaged a knuckle. From the way Corman shook his head, the blow must have stung. He turned with Murdock, glowering, waiting for the latter to settle and give him something to hit. Then, without warning, he sprang.

Murdock quickly gave ground, trying to avoid the heavy fists reaching to do damage. Too late he realized he had misjudged his position. Suddenly he found the edge of the bar against his back, and before he could sidestep away from it Tate Corman closed in on him and rocked him hard with a blow to the side of the head. His vision blurred. As a second heavy fist smashed him he felt a touch of panic. He tried to get his arms up but Corman had him pinned, helpless for the moment. He took a blow to the ribs that drove much of the wind from him.

The next moment the cheap wooden counter, insecurely anchored to the floor, tore loose with a screech of uprooted nails and toppled over ponderously against the back bar. Bottles and glassware slid off its shelves and smashed on the floor. Murdock was able to make his escape, rolling away from his enemy down the tilted slant of the bar front to end up on hands and knees.

He wanted only to find his wind and allow his head a moment to clear, but he wasn't given time; Corman's heavy boots were already coming after him. Murdock gathered himself and lunged sideways in a maneuver that caught the bigger man across the legs. Tripped up, Tate Corman tumbled heavily across him, and a boot toe struck him painfully in the ribs. Ben Murdock threw off his opponent's weight and managed to get his feet under him again.

A hand grabbed his arm; Lew Cotton was shouting, furious over the damage done to his bar. "Do you see what you're doing? Damn it, I want this stopped!" Murdock merely shook him off as Corman came lumbering up off the floor. At that moment the big man was wide open and Murdock hit him twice in the face and chest, stopping him in midstride. His head jerked back. When his knees buckled and he dropped, the sound as his skull struck the floor was distinctly audible.

Suddenly, at the sight of Tate Corman downed, the men who had crowded around the fighters fell totally silent, stunned. Murdock waited with the air sawing in and out of his lungs, feeling each punishing blow he had absorbed. He worked his aching fists and watched Corman pull himself painfully onto his elbows and remain there, head hanging and blood dripping to the floorboards. Murdock, sobbing for wind, managed to say hoarsely, "I'm ready to call it quits if you are, Tate."

The big man didn't seem to hear, nor did he make any attempt to lift his head or get up off the floor. Ben Murdock thought it must be clear to everyone, even his stoutest cronies, that Tate Corman had been beaten. He was not in much better shape himself. He lifted his hand to wipe a sleeve across his sweating and bloodied face, and at that instant something struck him, hard, at the base of the skull.

He had started to move just as the blow landed and it struck at an angle. Still, his head whipped forward with enough force to pop his neck, and one shoulder went instantly numb. For a heartbeat lamplight shattered into blackness, and he felt his knees begin to give way. Somehow he managed to keep from going down; with his head ringing he turned and saw Lew Cotton's bartender, arm raised and a bung starter in his fist.

The man looked at him with scared eyes. He had been carried away by excitement and probably had not really intended to hit the trail boss. He offered no resistance when Murdock snatched the implement from him and flung it aside, saying hotly, "That was a rotten thing to do! Couldn't you see the fight was over?"

Under his glare the bartender stammered incoherently, but the fellow's employer had no such trouble. Lew Cotton was furious, his face beet-red. "Don't *you* see the damage you've done?" he demanded. Ben Murdock, massaging the throbbing pain in neck and shoulder, looked at the bar, toppled and torn from its moorings, and the glittering shards of scattered glassware. He had to admit it looked almost as though a twister had struck the place. Amid the debris sat Tate Corman with head hanging, blood dripping from his face.

Murdock told the saloon owner curtly, "Add up the bill. It will be paid."

"It damn well better!" Cotton retorted. "If you Texans have got differences to settle, I'll thank you to take them somewhere else, not make a shambles out of my place of business!"

Murdock had no answer for that and he let it go. Already the noise in the room was building toward its previous level as those who were not concerned with the fight returned to their activities. Murdock walked over and stood above Corman, surrounded now by his friends. Both Finches were there, scowling at Murdock as the trail boss asked, "Will he be all right?" No one answered his question, but he doubted that the man he had beaten was seriously hurt. If anything, Murdock thought, he himself had probably taken the greater punishment.

Much as he regretted what had happened, he had at least vindicated himself in the eyes of those crew members who'd been waiting to see him stand up to big Tate Corman. As he went to join them, broken glass crunching underfoot, he was met with admiring grins and a slap on the shoulder that made him wince. Harry

Griffith shouted in his ear, "Great, boss! Great! You really put him in his place! By God, that was something to see!" Someone else said, "It had to be done. He wouldn't have it any other way!"

Ben Murdock, pulling on his hat, waved aside their compliments and said gruffly, "One thing we don't need is any more trouble. I suggest we clear out. There's other places along the street where they're going to be happier to see the likes of us."

Harry objected. "Hell, we seen what that sonofabitch of a bartender done to you when you wasn't looking. We ought to take the place apart!"

"Forget that!" Murdock said sternly. "The man simply lost his head. Besides, the place got took apart pretty well as it is. If you really want to do me a favor you'll all get out of here before somebody sends for the marshal and I have to argue with *him*. It wouldn't be worth it."

Some were in a mood to tackle the marshal as well, but they seemed more anxious to give Ben Murdock, their champion of the moment, what he asked for. They departed with boisterous talk and swagger after he got them headed for the door. They spilled out onto the porch, and he stood with the slatted doors behind him and watched them go tramping off in search of other saloons. Harry Griffith hung back long enough to ask anxiously, "You gonna let the doc look at that face, ain't you? Tate cut you up some with those fists of his."

Murdock said, "I'll be all right. But I'm counting on you, Harry, to keep the boys in line."

"Why, sure," the puncher said. "They won't be after

any trouble. They got too much to celebrate! Dab Pollard and Tate Corman, both getting what was overdue them—it was worth the trek to Kansas!"

Then he was gone, in the wake of the others. Looking across the batwings, Murdock saw that Cotton's was returning to normal. Some of the customers were helping to right the bar and repair what they could of the damage. One of the girls had a broom and was sweeping broken glassware. Yonder, Tate Corman was on his feet again and using the bar towel someone had handed him to mop the sweat and blood from his battered face.

Satisfied for now but weary to the bone, Ben Murdock turned away and walked alone to the hotel.

He had torn his new shirt and there was blood on it, though whether his own or Tate Corman's it would have been hard to say. In his room Murdock slipped out of the shirt, tossed it onto the foot of the metal bedstead, and dashed water from the basin over his sweaty torso. He seemed aware of every punished muscle. After he had dried himself he studied his face in the mirror. There was a fairly deep cut above his left eyebrow, and one cheek was puffed and tender, each separate tooth on that side of his jaw aching as though Corman's massive fist might have loosened them. Otherwise, although his head and shoulder hurt, he was less marked than he feared.

Murdock had asked at the desk for someone to bring warm water and now there was a knock on the door. He called out, "Come in," then turned and was a little embarrassed to see Amy Grover enter, a tin basin steaming in her hands and clean cloths across her arm. She didn't seem bothered to see him standing before her naked to the waist, and explained simply, "I was in the kitchen and heard about you being cut up in a fight. I offered to bring these up."

"Thank you, Amy. I appreciate your trouble."

He would have taken the things from her, but she shook her head. She peered with a look of concern at the marks on his face and said, "That's kind of a bad cut over your eye. Sit here and let me try to clean it up for you."

"It ain't necessary," he protested. "Really!"

But this girl who had been so timid and frightened of Jed Finch and his advances a little earlier appeared to have a will of her own. "Another person can do it for you easier than you can yourself," she pointed out. "And I'm not forgetting the way you helped me. Now, please!" And he found himself doing what she wanted, taking a chair by the table while she brought the lamp and placed it where it would give her good light.

Her brow was puckered and her face serious as she considered the damage Tate Corman's fists had done. She wet a corner of a towel and gently dabbed at the bloody tear above Murdock's eye, her head under its rich pile of brown hair tilted to one side. As she worked she asked hesitantly, "Was it the same man you had the trouble with earlier? You know, the—the one that—"

He didn't let her finish. "No, no, Amy," he told her. "This was someone else, and a different matter entirely.

121

You're not in any way responsible."

"I'm glad to know that. I'd have felt awful, thinking you'd been forced into a fight on account of me!"

Murdock frankly told her, "I wouldn't want you supposing I'm any kind of an angel. I've been in fights before, and I guess I've been the one that picked a few. But not tonight. I was doing my best to avoid this one. Can you believe that?"

"Of course," she answered readily. "Since you tell me so." And he found himself wondering why it had been important to know she thought his word was good.

She worked for a moment in silence. "You might have yourself a black eye," she said finally, "but I don't think it will be anything worse. I brought some iodine." She took it from a pocket of her apron. "I'd like to put some on that cut, but I'd better tell you it's apt to burn."

"Go ahead."

He tried to prevent it but the muscles of his cheeks bunched to the sting of the medicine; she noticed and her eyes showed sympathy. "All done," she said finally, and he thanked her.

Murdock took the towel, and as she watched him carefully use it she said suddenly, "I think Mr. Steadman said you're a drover. Is that different from a rancher?"

"Considerably," he told her. "A professional drover doesn't raise cattle; he makes a deal to deliver them to market for the men who do. Or if he has the capital, he puts together a shipping herd and hires and outfits a crew at his own expense. I hope to do that someday. So far the best I can manage is to hire out for wages as a trail boss. But one of these days I'll make it as a drover. I've promised myself!"

"A lot of responsibility, isn't it? And risk?"

He agreed as he turned to get his spare shirt and pull it on. "A dead end, too, I guess. Sooner or later this whole West is going to be crisscrossed with railroads, the way it is now east of the Mississippi. When that day comes the long drives will be over—and a good thing, I suppose. As it is now, we walk all the fat off a steer before we get him to market."

She asked, "What will *you* do afterwards?"

"Oh, I intend to stay in cattle," he said, buttoning the shirt. "Those same railroads will be opening new ranges—over Montana way and in Wyoming. Someday I mean to get my hands on some breeding stock and some land of my own. But that's all for the future."

She looked at him seriously. "If it's your dream, I sure hope it works out." She caught sight of the bloodied shirt hanging from the bedpost. She took it, saying, "I'll have this washed and ready for you in the morning. I see a tear that needs mending. . . ."

Murdock tried to protest. "You don't have to do all that." But she hung the shirt over an arm, assuring him, "I want to." She got the things she had brought with her, the water in the basin now tinged with his blood. "Good night," she said pleasantly, and a moment later was gone.

Murdock stood in the doorway and watched her descend the stairs, a trim figure in shirtwaist and skirt, a forthright and self-reliant girl who could still be honestly terrified of someone like Jed Finch. When her head with its crown of coiled brown hair disappeared below the level of the landing, Murdock turned back and closed the door on the stillness of the upper hallway, still thinking of her.

There was stillness outside his window, too. Murdock stood leaning with his palms upon the sill, looking down on the dark street. He knew he should be down there, keeping an eye on the uneasy peace and watching to see whatever happened when Tate Corman got over the worst effects of his beating. But for the moment he was too tired to move. His body needed rest, if only for a minute or two. He went over and let himself down on the edge of the bed, wondering when he would be able to afford the luxury of a night's sleep. He had earlier removed his spurs, and when he lay back, hoisting his boots onto the cheap bedspread, even the hard mattress felt fine to punished muscles. He let himself go loose, grateful to be able to enjoy a moment without any sort of urgency.

He was next aware of a hesitant rapping on the room's closed door. As he opened his eyes and blinked into the grainy light of early dawn, the knock was repeated and then the knob turned and the door cracked open. A voice he knew spoke to him in an urgent whisper. Shocked and fully awake, he exclaimed, "Rafael! What in the world . . . ?"

He pushed up, dropped his boots to the floor, and stared as the slim figure of the Mexican youth slipped through the doorway and approached his bed. Rafael was explaining hastily, "Señor Hoyt, he is ask I ride and find you if I can. He says try the hotel first. I don't see nobody downstairs but I find your name in the book, and your room number."

"Good thinking," Murdock said. "But what is it, Rafael? Something wrong at camp?"

"Is the herd," the jingler told him. "They have made—how you say? The estampede . . ."

Murdock stared at him. "Bad?"

"All across the flats."

The trail boss swore. Despite protesting muscles he was already on his feet, hurriedly taking his gunbelt down from the bedpost and buckling it on, grabbing up his hat and his spurs from the chair where he had left them. He asked quick questions and got answers from the Mexican: No, it didn't look like a bad run. The boys got right after it, aided by some who had returned to camp after an evening in town. Common sense indicated the cattle couldn't have run far; they should be easy enough to gather once they finished scattering over the wide river bottom and fell to grazing.

Murdock told himself he had no reason to feel guilty, having left things in the perfectly competent hands of Vern Hoyt. Still, he somehow felt responsible and was chagrined to remember how he had let himself stretch out on the bed last night—for a minute or two only—and then slept straight through until awakened by Rafael. A glance out the window revealed street dust streaked black with dew, the village sleeping in the predawn hush. Apparently the night here in town had been quiet enough after all.

But the next moment another question nagged at him. On such a night—with no wind to create threatening shadows in the brush, no lightning or thunder to startle them—why would a trail-weary herd, finally settled on a bedground, take it into their heads to run? Almost as though he'd put the question into words, he heard Rafael speaking behind him: "I don't know myself, but the boys, one or two, they say for sure they hear a gun go off. They say somebody has estart them critters!"

Murdock turned quickly from the window, his face hard. "That's all it would take, all right—one careless idiot with a gun! Any idea who? Or what he could have been shooting at?"

The slim youth shrugged. "I don't know, Señor Ben. Is all mixed up out there."

"I can imagine!" the trail boss grunted, and pulled on his hat. "My thanks for coming in to get me, Rafael. I'll fetch my horse from the livery and we'll go."

Dawn light was strengthening, the sun less than a quarter-hour below the horizon when they rode the murky river crossing and came out on the flats where the giant herd was feeding. There was little now to show there had been a run. Either it had been a very small one, or Vern Hoyt and his punchers had done an excellent job containing it. The first rider they met confirmed that everything was under control again. Murdock sent Rafael on to the wagons, in case George had need of him, and went looking for Hoyt.

He finally located his segundo. They reined in close and Murdock heard an account that was more detailed than the one he'd had from the Mexican. Hoyt, tense after the ordeal he had been put through, was relieved to see his boss. His fingers shook some as he rolled himself a smoke, but Murdock judged it was mostly from anger. Hoyt was furious. "By God, if I ever find out who it was had the itchy trigger finger," he promised darkly, "I'll personally make it hot for him! Lucky we ain't chasing this herd clear down the Arkansas!"

"Forget it," Murdock advised him. It was his guess someone had returned from town carrying a load of Eden Grove whiskey and too befuddled to think. Since he wasn't apt to step forward, it was unlikely they would ever pin the blame. "Let's be glad it wasn't any worse. The herd seems quiet enough now. What do you say we ride in to the fire and see if George has some coffee boiling. . . ."

Hoyt stared at him; only now was he taking a good look at his boss. "For the love of Mike!" he exclaimed. "What did you do to yourself?"

"*I* didn't do it," Murdock said, putting a hand to the discolored and painful lacerations his segundo was staring at. Apparently no news of the fight with Tate Corman had as yet reached Hoyt. As they rode across the bottoms toward the wagon camp Murdock gave a brief account of it.

The news jarred the other free from his single-minded concern with the herd. "Dab Pollard—picked like a chicken! And Corman cut down to size! And I had to miss all that!" He shook his head. "I ain't so sure, though," he added darkly, "that we've heard the last of it. Tate Corman ain't the man to take a licking. This is only going to make him sorer than ever. Get him sore enough, I wouldn't lay any bets as to what he might do."

Murdock didn't comment.

The sun was up by now, and the day's white heat already beginning to shimmer across the flats, turning the river to a dazzle. At the wagons men moved woodenly, some looking hungover and bleary-eyed from interrupted sleep. As he and Murdock dismounted and headed for the fire and the blackened coffee pot, Vern Hoyt remarked, "The boys who stayed out last night to get the bonus more than earned it. It's time we got some of the others back so's the rest can have their turn in town."

"I'll see to it."

Taking his time over the blistering-hot liquid in his tin coffee cup, the trail boss watched George stomping around the wagon, going about his interminable chores. The cook was always a short-tempered man but this morning his mood seemed blacker than ordinary. When Murdock heard the way he turned on a puncher who came to ask a perfectly innocent question, he felt he had to put in a word. "George," he called to the old man. "What's eating you? I've never seen a chip like you got on your shoulder this morning."

"Oh, you ain't?" George snapped back at him. "Well, damned if I ain't of a mind to call it quits with this outfit! It ain't enough that I'm expected to feed a mob the size of this one—and without being shown the kind of respect I got a right to!"

Vern Hoyt, used to the cook's grumbling, swallowed a smile. "So what is it this time? What's happened now?"

"Maybe you think it's funny?" the old man retorted. "I'll have you know I got feelings, and right now I got a skull that's like an eggshell somebody scrunched open!"

"You, George? I didn't even know you was a drinking man."

"I ain't, damn it! I been doing nothing but mind my own business. If I'd done it better, this might not have happened to me."

"What did happen?" Murdock asked him. "You still haven't told us."

"Why, somebody slugged me, *that's* what!" the cook said. "Sometime after that fool gunshot went off. I knew, once the excitement was over, the boys would be after me and setting up a yell for coffee, so I was just fixing it when I heard somebody sneaking around the wagons. Well, naturally I went charging over to tell him to get the hell out there with the herd where he belonged—and damned if my skull didn't run into a gunbarrel! By time my head cleared, the bastard was gone. And that's what I get, trying to do the owners a favor!" He put a hand to his head and winced. Ben Murdock, who was still feeling the effects of a bung starter in the hands of Lew Cotton's bartender, could sympathize.

Hoyt, too, was beginning to take the matter more seriously. "Tell us who it was, George, and we'll see he answers for this."

129

George made an irritable gesture. "How can I? It was pitch dark. I never seen his face. He didn't say a word—just let me have it. I tell you, it had to have been a gunbarrel."

"You say this was near the wagon?" All at once a thought pulled Ben Murdock off the cottonwood log where he had been seated; he put aside his tin coffee cup as he stood. "Maybe you'd better show us. . . ."

Still grumbling, George led them around to the far side of the chuckwagon, where water for a dry drive was carried in two barrels lashed to the timbers. During all the weeks on the trail it had been carefully hoarded, but now, with the river less than a mile away, the men had become careless and a good deal had been allowed to spill out to make a black expanse of slop and mud.

Vern Hoyt said, "For all you can say, maybe this fellow only stopped to get a drink before setting out to help with the beef."

"But why did he have to go and hit me?" George demanded. "If he didn't figure he was doing something he shouldn't . . ."

There were boot tracks all around the wagon. What attracted Ben Murdock's attention was a pair that indicated someone had sunk deep into the mud, almost to his ankles; even the marks left by large-roweled spurs showed plainly. He eyed them, then stared thoughtfully at the wagon. "Have you looked inside?" he asked suddenly.

The cook scowled. "What for?"

The wagon's rear end was occupied by a storage cabinet of many sections, especially built for it, the lowered tailgate serving as a work table. Murdock wasn't interested in this. He went up the wheel and over the front seat, into the area of the wagon box that was filled with sacks of beans and coffee and flour. There, in the light of morning sun filtered through canvas, he found what he was looking for. He climbed out and showed it to Vern Hoyt and the cook—a metal cash box, its lid forced, empty.

"Obviously this is what he was after," Murdock said. "He knew where it was kept; he rifled it and pocketed the money. You can see the marks where he jumped down into the mud—no other way he could make prints that deep. He'd tried to clear everybody out of camp by firing off a gun and starting the herd running. When he saw somebody coming he didn't take any chances—he pole-axed George, and lit out."

Staring, Hoyt swore under his breath. "Sonofabitch! You're saying it was somebody who *knew* where Sherm Watkins kept the cash fund? Then it would of had to be one of the crew; but, which? And more important, with the headstart he's got, how far has he gone by this time?"

"Not too far," Murdock assured him. "I'll be going along now to pick him up. Vern, I'd like you riding with me—I might need you for a witness."

Hoyt wasted no more time with questions. "Sure, Ben," he grunted. "I'm ready whenever you are. . . ."

CHAPTER IX

Townsmen are notoriously late risers. Though it was well after seven o'clock, Eden Grove seemed scarcely to have come alive. In the still air, smoke from breakfast fires stood like pillars above a dozen chimneys, but except for Duffy's restaurant—open to catch any early trade—the business houses along Railroad Avenue stood closed in the slanting morning sunlight, with only a couple of horses standing forlornly, as though forgotten, at the rails along the four-block length of the street. Riding in, Hoyt and Murdock were nearly alone in the morning stillness.

The door of the mercantile stood open and a woman in an apron with a cloth tied about her hair was using a broom. She stopped and straightened a moment, looking at the silent street and at the two horsemen approaching from the river crossing. Murdock had heard that the store manager, Harolday, had a young and attractive wife; obviously the reports were true.

She turned back into the building, taking her broom but leaving the door open to let out the night's trapped mustiness. Her departure left one other person visible on the street, a man who paraded alone up and down in front of the closed entrance to Cotton's saloon. Though none of these places were open yet, he had managed to promote a bottle of whiskey somewhere. As he moved jerkily to and fro he talked to himself and paused frequently to tilt the bottle in his hand and take a drag from it. It looked as though he had already downed a good half of its contents.

Murdock and Hoyt exchanged meaningful glances, and without comment reined toward him. They halted their horses and sat looking at him a moment before the trail boss spoke. "Well, Pollard, looking for some action? You may have to wait; everything appears to be closed."

On the sidewalk, Dab Pollard looked around at them, blinking in surprise. He didn't appear much like himself this morning—hatless and unkempt, his usual arrogance missing. "I'm looking for that tinhorn—that Kimbrough," he said loudly. "Bastard owes me a game. Last night he said anytime."

"He meant any time within reason. And he told you you'd have to have a stake."

Vern Hoyt said, "Sure—I heard he plumb cleaned you out."

"Don't worry about *me,*" Pollard assured them boldly. "I got my stake, all right."

He took another pull on his bottle. Taken on what was probably an empty stomach, the whiskey had him well on his way to drunkenness. Murdock, observing the man with sour distaste, decided he might as well get this over with. "Have you taken a look at your boots?" he demanded. "Where'd you have got into mud like that? Clean up to your ankles . . ." Pollard stared at him blankly, and then down at his feet as though mystified to find the well-scuffed cowhides caked with dried gumbo.

"You didn't even know, did you?" the trail boss went

133

on relentlessly. "I guess I'll just have to tell you, then. It happened during the night, at camp—when you jumped down into that slop next the wheel of the chuckwagon. That was just before George stumbled onto you, and you had to pistolwhip him!"

The look in Pollard's eyes suddenly changed. If he was partly drunk, he was still sober enough to recognize danger. His whole expression seemed to narrow down. Stalling for time while he got his startled thoughts in order, he said hoarsely, "I don't know what you're talking about!"

"The hell you don't!" Murdock's revelation had jarred the words out of Vern Hoyt. "You lying sonofabitch . . ."

Pollard's veneer of pretense crumbled. Moving faster than anyone would have expected, he flung the bottle he had been drinking from straight at the man who accused him. Murdock jerked his head out of the way. The bottle was still in the air, winking reflected sunlight and trailing a stream of amber whiskey, when Pollard caught up the sixshooter in his holster and flung a shot at Murdock.

The bullet went wide, for Pollard was already spinning away as he fired. Vern Hoyt loosed a startled shout. The next instant Pollard was running full tilt along the street.

Murdock swore and gave his horse a kick, pursuing with Hoyt close behind him. The fugitive, hearing horses pounding up, knew there was no hope of outdistancing them. He threw a frantic look around him. He had reached the door of the grocery, left open when the woman finished her sweeping. Pollard didn't hesitate. He braked, whirled, and ducked into the sanctuary of the doorway, pausing there long enough to let another blind shot at his pursuers smash the morning stillness. Then he plunged inside and the door slammed shut behind him.

Lucy Harolday, kneeling to polish the glass front of a showcase, stared at the intruder. He demanded harshly, "Is there a back way out of here?" but she gave no sign she had even heard the question. Pollard wasted no time on her. He had already seen the curtained doorway at the rear, and without further pause he started for it.

The curtain was suddenly whipped aside and he was confronted by Sam Harolday. The two men looked at each other. Dab Pollard brought up his gun, pointed it at the storekeeper's head, and said harshly, "You get out of my way!"

Harolday looked at the gun's muzzle, still dribbling smoke. He looked at the distorted face behind it, and then glanced at his wife who remained on her knees, frightened and unmoving, with a hand pressed against her cheek. Harolday was as pale as his own shirtfront, but in spite of the gun something gave him courage enough to stand his ground, and his jaw became rigid as he answered, "No!"

Pollard's face was terrible. "You think I won't use this?"

"I only know that you're not going back there. It's

135

our home; our little girl is there. I won't have her frightened out of her wits!'"

For all his haste Dab Pollard hesitated. Perhaps he couldn't understand someone who would actually face a smoking gun with his own hands empty; or perhaps, in that moment, he perceived a strength in the character of Sam Harolday that matched the stern set of his features. But then it was too late for Pollard. Amid shouting voices outside and a trample of boots, the street door was flung open and two men burst through. Harolday forgotten, the fugitive whirled around, but before he could make a move to use his gun Murdock and Hoyt were on top of him.

Ben Murdock concentrated on capturing the weapon and keeping Pollard's muddled reflexes from loosing any wild bullets. He missed in his grab for the man's gun hand, caught the barrel and had his fingers torn by the front sight as Dab Pollard tried to twist free. The next moment Pollard managed to shake off the older Vern Hoyt, and swung a fist that took Murdock in the chest and staggered him. The trail boss caught himself, and with Pollard's whiskey-laden breath panting in his face he managed to grab the other's shoulder, whirl him about, and get an armlock from behind. The gun got away from him, but he caught Pollard's sleeve and slammed his wrist twice against a counter's edge. With the second blow the man grunted in pain, his fingers flew open, and the gun popped loose.

"Now, will you cut it out?" Ben Murdock said.

Pollard was in no mood to give up yet. Breathing hard with the effort, he continued to buck and struggle

136

until Vern Hoyt located the fallen sixshooter, snatched it up, and shoved the muzzle of it against the man's ribs. That seemed to shock the fight out of him. He suddenly became still, and Ben Murdock said gruffly, "That's better! Now try and show some sense!"

"What's going on here?" a voice demanded.

It was Sherm Watkins at the door. "What's going on?" he repeated as he stared at the three Pool crewmen—two holding a third one prisoner. "What was that shooting? Has this man been up to something?"

Sam Harolday spoke up. "He came charging in here and threatened my wife and me with a gun!"

"We were after him," Murdock said. "He was only trying to get away. Now turn around," he ordered. "Put your hands on that counter top and lean on them!" Face red and scowling, Dab Pollard let himself be pushed into position. Then, while Vern Hoyt kept the gun on him, Murdock slapped the pockets of his clothing and quickly came up with a roll of greenbacks which he dropped upon the counter. "Take a look," he invited, motioning to Watkins.

The Pool rancher closed the door, walked over, and poked at the money with a finger, spreading it out upon the counter top as Murdock explained about Dab Pollard's losses in the poker game of last night; about the gunshot that started a stampede and drew off the men of the trail camp while the box where Watkins kept the herd funds was rifled; about the clubbing of George. . . .

"It's a lie!" Pollard broke in. "All of it! This money

137

belongs to me—you can't prove it don't!"

"You sure?" Sherm Watkins pulled a greenback out of the scatter and held it up so they all could see it was a five-dollar bill with one torn end. "When I paid off the crew last evening I couldn't find a man in the outfit who'd take this as part of his wages, no matter that I told them it was perfectly good. I had to end up putting it back in the cash box. I know only one way Pollard could have it on him now!"

"You got an answer for *that?*" Vern Hoyt asked the prisoner harshly. Pollard said nothing. He had fallen glumly silent, but a muscle in his jaw was working sporadically. He was a changed man suddenly, the arrogance wiped out of him. A gleam of sweat shone on his cheek.

Watkins addressed the storekeeper. "I apologize to you and your missus. I want you to know this man don't work for me—but I'll be willing to pay if there's damage."

"No damage, I guess." Harolday looked at his wife for confirmation. He appeared a little shaken; possibly he only now realized the risk he had taken, standing up to a drunken man with a gun in his fist. His manner was strained as he told the Pool rancher, "Just get him out of here. And keep him out!"

"Certainly." Watkins gathered and pocketed the stolen money. "Bring him along," he ordered the ones who held the prisoner, and went to open the door for them. Murdock and Vern Hoyt each caught their man by an arm, but Pollard had turned belligerent again. "Where you taking me?" he cried in alarm. He tried to hold back, but despite his struggles Hoyt and Murdock hustled him out through the door. Spurs rang on the dry sidewalk planking as he fought to get free. Sherm Watkins lent a hand for a moment, then in exasperation told Vern Hoyt, "We've had enough of this! Fetch a rope."

The nearest available was on Hoyt's own saddle, and in going for it he had to shove a couple of bystanders out of his path—all at once a crowd had started to gather. When Dab Pollard saw the rope he lost his head completely. "You're gonna string me up!" he shouted, hysteria in his voice. "For nothing more than—"

"Oh, shut up!" Sherm Watkins hauled the prisoner's arms around behind him, but at the actual touch of the hemp at his wrists Pollard went wild again, screaming and fighting as Watkins expertly made his wrap and tie. Even with his hands pinioned the man was impossible to subdue, and the crowd in the street seemed to swell with the excitement. A cur dog came darting from somewhere and began nipping and snarling at the heels of the men, worrying them but somehow managing to avoid their kicks.

Suddenly an elbow thrust into Vern Hoyt's middle partially winded him and sent him staggering, giving Dab Pollard a chance to break free. Pollard had glimpsed a friend in the crowd and yelled, "Tate! Tate, do something! *They want to hang me!*" But when he started for Tate Corman his heel caught in a rut and he went down into the street dust. With his hands tied behind him he floundered, unable to get up again. He made it as far as his knees, but by that time Sherm

Watkins had captured the end of the rope and Vern Hoyt, with a boot at the dog's ribs that sent it yelping, reached Pollard and hauled him to his feet.

Hoyt was still panting for wind. "Will you stop it!" he exclaimed angrily. "Nobody's talking about anybody getting hanged, but you keep this up and I might be tempted!" A couple of loops of the rope pinned the prisoner's arms to his body and made him finally quiet down.

Dab Pollard didn't look much like the arrogant manipulator of stacked decks who had challenged his victims to make the most of his cheating. He peered around wildly, hair glued to his face with sweat, and there was a frantic appeal for help in the look he gave Tate Corman. The latter came striding up with his friends behind him and demanded in a voice that carried above the noise in the street, "What the hell's going on?"

It was Ben Murdock who told him roughly, "Keep your distance, Tate. This man is in custody." Corman, he was interested to see, bore his share of damage from last night's mauling in the saloon. A cheek was swollen and the eye above it nearly closed. But Murdock was wary, knowing that pain and the memory of defeat would make the big man's temper more uncertain than ever.

Corman had the two Finch brothers with him and a couple of Wilson Stiles riders. They listened with thunderous belligerence as Murdock briefly outlined the charges against the prisoner—the stampede, the looted cash box, the attack on George. "Who you expect to believe that kind of a yarn?" interrupted Tate Corman.

"It's not a yarn," Sherm Watkins assured him. "The money was in his pocket."

"Money one of you likely planted there!"

The Pool owner stiffened. "Now you just hold on, Corman. . . ."

Emboldened, Dab Pollard started yelling again: "Tate, they're trying to frame me! They hate all us Stiles men—they always have. They want to string me up for no reason!"

"Nonsense!" Watkins snapped. "We know you're guilty as hell, but so far nobody's made up their minds *what* should be done with you."

"I'll tell you what you can do," said Corman. "You can turn him loose. Right now!"

"Back off, Tate!" Ben Murdock could feel his own temper beginning to slip. As he spoke his warning and brought Corman's eyes to him, he saw a slow flush begin to crawl its way over the big man's features. Resentful because of the beating he had taken the previous evening, Tate Corman would probably be glad to renew their fight, on any slight pretext, at any moment, and it looked as though Jed Finch and the others at his back were all too ready to egg him on.

Behind Murdock, Harry Griffith said suddenly, "Don't let him bluff you out, boss! Hell, that crowd's been pushing for trouble ever since we left Texas. If they want a showdown, maybe it's time we gave 'em one!"

Sherm Watkins told his rider sharply, "You stay out of this, Harry!" But when Murdock looked around he

141

could see that the puncher wasn't speaking only for himself. The two factions stood confronted; in the next few moments anything might happen.

A hot wind swept the street, filling the air with glittering dust and buffeting them all, but no one moved. No one seemed willing to take his eyes off the other group. Then the dust fell back, and out of its settling cloud strode Jay Gerringer.

The marshal's hands hung empty. The morning sun made a dazzle of the polished metal pinned to the lapel of his coat as he walked out into the space separating the two groups of hostile Texans. He told them crisply, "I don't know what's in your heads, but any one of you who touches a gun is going to have it taken away from him! You had better all believe that!"

He stood and sent his cold stare over their faces, letting the statement sink in. Lastly he singled out Tate Corman. "What about you?" he prompted, bearing down. Corman's bruised lips moved soundlessly. Ben Murdock saw his chest swell, but then a movement of the heavy shoulders indicated that Wilson Stiles's foreman had given way.

Jay Gerringer read the signs and gave him no further attention. Addressing the whole group, he went on in the same tone: "It doesn't matter in the least to me what might be splitting this trail outfit. Just understand that you will not bring your differences into town with you—not while I'm wearing the star."

"That's the thing I'm trying to prevent," Watkins assured him.

"I'm pleased to hear it." Gerringer looked at Dab

Pollard, who stood with his arms tied by the rope in Watkins' hands. "As for this man, it appears he stands accused of theft, and assault and battery. That being a matter for the law, I'll take him off your hands."

Watkins nodded, clearly all too happy to let him. The easiest thing would have been to go along, but Ben Murdock saw a problem, and however reluctantly he had to say, "I'm afraid you can't do that, Marshal. Even supposing you had a jail to hold him in."

"Oh?" The lawman's head turned slowly, and the corrosive stare of those deepset eyes rested on Murdock. "Tell me why not," the man said, a shade too quietly.

"I'd think it was obvious. You're a town officer. It ain't your authority to arrest him for something that happened over there, across the river."

For a long moment he endured the weight of that stare. "You seem pretty free about explaining my business!" Gerringer said finally. "What would be *your* idea? You want to take him in to the sheriff's office and then wait around Hutchinson a month or two, for the circuit judge to sit on his case?"

Murdock had no ready answer, and there was no need for one. Sherm Watkins had been listening, and now the Pool rancher said, "I see no call for that. We got the money back; there's nothing to gain from pressing charges. Vern, which bronc was Pollard riding?"

Vern Hoyt jerked a thumb toward a horse that stood at a nearby tie rack. "The knothead gray yonder, I guess. It's part of Stiles's string."

"It'll do. Fetch it up." As Hoyt, with a puzzled shrug, turned to make his way through the crowd and get the animal, Sherm Watkins set to work undoing the rope that held the prisoner. "I'm turning you loose, Pollard," the rancher said. "You ain't worth the trouble it would be trying to hold onto you, or get you the punishment you deserve—though if you'd actually busted George's skull, I can tell you it would be an entirely different story. Take the gray and get out! You ain't wanted any longer around this outfit. You're to stay clear away from the herd, and away from camp." The rope fell away. As Pollard sullenly rubbed his wrists, something in the look of him infuriated Sherm Watkins, who seized him by a shoulder and spun him around. "Are you listening to me?"

Pollard met his look. "There's stuff that belongs to me," he said in sullen defiance. "My warbag and my bedroll, at the wagon . . ."

"All right." Watkins dropped his hand. "You can stop off and pick them up, but make sure you don't waste any time about it. I'll see that the crew is put on notice you ain't allowed to 'light. We none of us ever want to lay eyes on you again!"

Dab Pollard could only glare. Tate Corman felt called on for a blustering protest. "Sherm, who the hell do you think you are, giving orders like that?"

"I'm giving them!" Watkins answered. He told Murdock, "You're to see the crew gets the word."

Ben Murdock nodded. He was genuinely surprised. Watkins was never a man he would have looked to for firmness. But Corman wasn't finished. "I promise you now," he said loudly, "you can't make this stick! The man ain't part of your crew, Watkins. He rides for Stiles, and ain't anybody else can fire him. I reckon Stiles will have something to say about this, all right, when he gets back from Ellsworth."

"I'll worry about that when he does. I don't know what he *can* say after he hears about last night! There's your horse," Watkins told the prisoner, and gave Pollard a shove as Vern Hoyt came up, leading it by the reins. "Get on him."

Jay Gerringer had something to add to that. "You have five minutes," he said when the man gave no sign of obeying. "Just that long to be out of Eden Grove or face a vagrancy charge. If your own outfit won't have you, then this town certainly doesn't need you either."

To Ben Murdock, it seemed a matter of touch and go at that moment. Tempers were close to the flash point—Pollard's friends furious at what was being done to him, his enemies angry at seeing him let off. Murdock was trying to keep an eye on everything at once as the accused man jerked the reins from Vern Hoyt, fumbled at the stirrup and pulled himself into the saddle.

Even now, Pollard wasn't ready to go without a final shot. The horse moving uneasily about under him, he put a glowering stare on Sherm Watkins. In a trembling voice, he said, "Don't be too sure this is the end of it! There could be another day."

"There better not be," Vern Hoyt answered for the Pool owner. "Not if you know what's good for you!"

Murdock thought he knew a weak bluff when he saw

145

it. Watkins, with fists on hips and head to one side, met the glare of the man in the saddle and made a promise of his own: "Mister, I'm going to see to it personally that every rancher in the Pool hears this story. Before I get through, you can take it for gospel there ain't an outfit back home that'll be inclined to give you any kind of a job. You can do yourself a favor if you don't bother to show your face around that part of the world again!"

"Hell, man!" Tate Corman exploded. "You can't close the whole state of Texas to him!" Jed Finch added, "By God, he can have a job with *me*. All he has to do is ask!"

Sherm Watkins shook his head. "You really mean this? Finch, I kind of doubt you'd want to risk your standing with the Pool, taking in somebody like him."

Jed Finch opened his mouth and then closed it, and his face turned several different shades. Sherm Watkins had correctly read his bluff and called it, and Murdock knew the man was thinking twice. Where he was concerned, being accepted as a member of the Pool outweighed anything else.

Vern Hoyt told the man in the saddle, "You've about used up your five minutes. . . ."

A tirade of cursing answered him, but there was nothing left in Dab Pollard now except weak bluster and he was drowned out by catcalls from his numerous enemies in the crowd. Beaten, he yanked the gray's head around and gave it a furious kick with a big-roweled spur. Right now he seemed to want nothing more than to get away from there. As he kicked his horse into a dust-raising start and headed west, the cowboys poured into the street and waved and hooted him out of sight.

CHAPTER X

The lonely whistle of the morning work train, approaching Eden Grove on its way to the end of the track, sounded over the broad Arkansas bottoms. It found Ben Murdock making his way across the flats, assessing the amount of drift among the Pool herd after last night's run and overseeing his crew in pulling them back together. He reined in where he had a glimpse of the steel rails beyond the river, and presently was rewarded with the sight of a smoke trail and then of the engine itself. It looked almost like a toy from this distance, as it puffed busily up the valley. The train consisted chiefly of flatcars loaded with rails and timbers and other materials, but there were also a couple of boxcars, undoubtedly headed for the switch at Eden Grove, and a single passenger coach.

As the morning sun flashed off the coach windows, Murdock thought again of Phil Steadman's promise to have a buyer on this train. A lot was riding on it, including Murdock's justification for insisting they bring the herd to a place no one had seen before. He watched the engine, already slowing for the trestle east of town, its bell echoing thinly, and he could picture Sherm Watkins waiting impatiently in the crowd at the depot. If no buyer appeared, he knew he could expect some very heavy discussion later on.

So he had a definite feeling of relief when he returned to the wagons an hour later and saw Watkins and another man approaching from the direction of the river. He let himself believe that he knew who Watkins' companion was. The stranger's clothing, and the way he sat the horse he'd borrowed from the livery, indicated he was no cattleman. Murdock was down and waiting when the pair came to a halt, and without dismounting the Pool rancher made introductions.

"Paul Chadwick here is the man Steadman was telling us about—represents a K.C. packing firm."

"And you're the one who delivered five thousand Texas longhorns?" Chadwick reached a hand down from the saddle. "That was something to undertake."

"I had help," Murdock said, as he shook the hand. Paul Chadwick's hand was without calluses but his grip was firm. He was cleanshaven and direct of eye, a man who would be attractive to women.

Sherm Watkins suggested, "How about a cup of coffee all around, and something to eat? Then we'll go look at some cattle."

The buyer was agreeable to that, and they dismounted.

Over their tin cups and plates they exchanged gossip of the trail and of the market towns. Murdock, who knew better than to expect Chadwick to reveal his hand by discussing prices and conditions before actual dickering began, was content to ask about people he had met in other years at Ellsworth and Abilene. Since the latter town had taken itself out of the Texas trade,

Chadwick said, the railroads were as concerned as anyone about establishing new shipping points. Longhorn beef was important to them since it satisfied the need for a cargo to load for the East, instead of having to return empty after satisfying a voracious appetite for supplies resulting from the opening of the Plains. He had seen Eden Grove once before, a few short weeks ago, and now declared himself astonished at the way the town had grown. He predicted it would have a prosperous future.

But Sherm Watkins, a Texan with little interest in the future of a Kansas community, soon grew impatient with the talk and suggested they get on with the business of looking over a herd for sale. Chadwick agreed, and small talk was forgotten. As they returned to their saddles they had the air of men about to involve themselves in the important business of dickering.

Murdock rode along but kept his distance. As trail boss his only part in this was to answer questions and give orders for any particular animals to be brought up for the buyer's closer inspection as they made a leisurely tour of the mammoth herd. Watkins was a careful dealer and a fair one. He pointed out that in a herd this size, made up of many separate brands, there had to be stock of differing quality. Paul Chadwick took this without comment. He kept his cards well hidden and his thoughts to himself until he was ready to air them.

Then abruptly he declared himself satisfied. He drew rein, took out a handkerchief, and mopped his face and the sweatband of his hat. He said, "There are some poor-looking animals here that by rights should be culled out, but I won't make an issue of it and I won't quibble. I've seen smaller herds that didn't end the drive in as good shape; five thousand head in one bunch is worth making some concessions. I'll buy the entire herd just as it stands. I'll take your count, and I'll pay eighteen a head. I can promise you won't get a better deal this season anywhere in Kansas."

Murdock knew he spoke the simple truth. It was a good price, advantageous to the Pool because it disposed of the entire herd in one transaction without the need of weeding out certain animals or bargaining with many buyers, and also to Paul Chadwick's backers since it meant filling a lot of contracts with a single purchase. Sherm Watkins plainly agreed, and it was with reluctance that he told the other man, "Sounds fair enough to me; I only wish I was in a position to settle the matter right now. I got eight hundred head under my own brand that you can sure as hell have on those terms. Trouble is, you want them all, and it so happens I ain't able to make that kind of a deal."

He proceeded to explain about the Pool, a majority of its members having voted Wilson Stiles authority to negotiate for all of them in the sale of the big herd.

"You say the man's gone to Ellsworth?" Chadwick was frowning. "You might have told me! It's a strange way to do business—taking up my time to look at a herd and then not allowing me to make a bid on it!"

"Nobody intended it this way," Watkins said lamely. "I was hoping Stiles would of showed up before now. If you'll give him a few more hours . . ."

The cattle buyer spoke stiffly. "I can't wait. I have to be on the next train back to Wichita. Too bad, too; we could have done business." He picked up the reins. About to pull away, he hesitated as though reluctant to break off negotiations. "Look, you have my bid," he told Sherm Watkins. "Even if this man of yours turns up with a better one, I think I should at least be given the right to match it. Get a wire to me inside twenty-four hours; otherwise, we'll have to forget the whole matter."

The Pool rancher agreed to that quickly enough, but there was considerable chilliness in the air as Paul Chadwick took his leave with little more than a nod. Silently watching him ride away across the grass, Ben Murdock could easily guess how Sherm Watkins felt after almost closing a $90,000 deal and then seeing it come to nothing. Murdock thought he had no choice but to say, "It was my fault, for letting things come to a breaking point between me and Wilson Stiles. Otherwise he'd be here now, and you'd have had your deal."

Watkins, as though not trusting himself to answer, merely shrugged and turned his horse toward the wagons. But there was little doubt where he laid the blame.

Some bleak thoughts occurred to Murdock an hour later as he rode across the flats toward the river crossing and the raw buildings of the village. Whatever he thought of Wilson Stiles, he told himself, it had been foolish to let his anger at the man override his own best interests. Not only had he created difficulties for himself on this particular drive; he could have damaged the reputation he was trying to build as a reliable trail boss. His whole career could suffer if he couldn't keep his feelings under better control than that!

But then he remembered Stiles's cool indifference concerning the fate of Wally McKay, who could have died for all he cared. Ben Murdock shook his head and said aloud, "No, by God! Somebody had to call his hand! *Somebody* had to tell the bastard off proper!" And having got that off his chest—knowing that if he had to he'd do exactly the same again—he found he felt considerably better.

A rising wind blew against him with an oven breath, running in waves through the flattened grasses of the river bottom. Clouds he hadn't noticed before were massing low along the horizon; here on the plains, they might bring a storm or they might mean nothing. If heavy weather did develop there could be another watchful night ahead for the men who tended the big herd. He was considering that as he hauled up to wait, buffeted by wind-flung grit and cinders, while another work train crawled by without pausing at the depot and rolled on toward end of track, bell stroking and the noise of the steam jets echoing off the building fronts. Murdock crossed behind the caboose, lifting a hand in salute to a brakeman who lounged in the car's rear door. He rode directly to the grocery and general store and there dismounted.

He had a short list of supplies George had asked him to pick up; it was one of his reasons for riding in from camp. Entering the store he found Mrs. Harolday and her daughter, who was playing quietly in the corner, making a bed out of an empty crate for an old rag doll. Murdock handed over the order to be filled, explaining that he had other business and would be around later for it. She could put it on the bill Sherm Watkins had opened.

Watching Lucy Harolday glance over the list—looking at her pale hair with its center part like a ruled line, the faint sheen of moisture on her face due to the breathless heat—he felt he couldn't leave without telling her, "I've been wanting to apologize, Mrs. Harolday. For the trouble this morning. Murdock's the name."

She lifted unfriendly eyes. "Well, Mr. Murdock, it *was* one of your men that came breaking in on us. . . ."

"Not one of *my* men," he corrected her. "I'm only the trail boss. But I'm still sorry about it. I hope the little girl wasn't upset any."

"Jeanie?" Hearing her name, the child promptly got to her feet and came trotting over to press against her mother's long skirt. The woman laid a hand upon the head that was so like her own. The little girl considered Murdock in a manner as calm and contained as her mother's. "I assure you," Lucy Harolday said evenly—though he thought he detected a note of bitterness—"since we came to this town Jeanie has heard enough guns, and enough shouting from drunken men, that nothing of that sort is likely to bother her."

Frowning, he said, "You must have known the kind of place you'd be bringing her into. . . . It would help, of course, if you'd keep her away from Railroad Avenue."

"It happens the store is our home—the only one we have. My husband was employed as manager by the men who built Eden Grove."

"Beason and Colby, you mean?"

She nodded. "And now, suddenly, they're gone, and everything's confused—and nobody seems to know who it is my husband's working for. Until the courts decide, we must simply hang on and do the best we can."

"Yes, ma'am." He found her willingness to discuss her personal affairs with a stranger somewhat disconcerting. "Well, I wish you luck," he said a little gruffly. "And again, I'm sorry about this morning. At least I can say nobody's apt to have more trouble from that fellow Pollard. We haven't seen hide or hair of him since he was ordered out of town."

About to leave, Murdock hesitated at a glass-front display case that held a few boxes of cheap penny candy. On an impulse he said, "Can I buy the little girl something? I see a stick of licorice there; looks like it would taste good."

"Jeanie isn't allowed candy," her mother told him. "Only on special occasions."

"I just found a nickel in my pocket," Murdock said, and fished it out. "That's a special occasion." He placed the coin on top of the case and looked inquiringly at the woman. "May I?"

Jeanie Harolday said nothing but her eyes were dancing. Even Lucy Harolday's frosty exterior melted a trifle, and she even smiled. "Oh, all right."

"Good!" He shoved the nickel toward her. "Have her pick out whatever she likes best."

"I will." To her daughter she said, "Thank Mr. Murdock."

"Thank you, Mr. Murdock," the little girl said gravely.

"You're more than welcome, Jeanie." With a glance at her mother he touched his hatbrim, and left.

Outside he encountered Harry Griffith. Harry had been, at last, to the barber. His head was shorn high and pale above the ears and across the neck, changing its shape completely, and as he came along the boardwalk he trailed a cloud of bay rum that caused Ben Murdock's nose to wrinkle. Harry saw his expression and went instantly on the defensive. "It cost me two bits," he pointed out irritably. "So I was gonna see to it I got my money's worth—the works!"

Murdock hid his amusement. He said, "I take it, then, things are no longer on the house this morning. Well, it was too good to last; the town's here to make money off the likes of us, and you can't blame them for getting down to business sooner or later." Getting down to business himself, he added, "Have you seen Tate Corman?"

"I think I seen him go into the restaurant a few minutes ago."

"Thanks."

Harry gave him an anxious warning. "If you're looking for him, you better watch out. After all that's been happening Tate's in kind of a dangerous mood!"

"So am I," Murdock said shortly. "Let Tate Corman watch out!"

"Maybe I better come along."

Murdock started to refuse, then changed his mind. "All right, Harry. But only because I may have a chore for you."

He left his horse in front of the mercantile, and with Harry Griffith walked the short distance to the New York Restaurant. There, on stools along the counter, they found Corman flanked by Pike Finch and the Finch hand, Gater. It was the latter who first became aware of the newcomers, and he nudged Corman with an elbow. Corman twisted about, jaw bulging and fork poised. He said gruffly around a mouthful of food, "What do *you* want?"

His tone of voice caused Duffy, the proprietor, to turn from the sink behind the counter where he was washing dirty dishes.

Ben Murdock was determined not to match Corman's hostility. Harry Griffith retorted loudly, "Maybe we came in to eat—if it's any business of yours!" but Murdock cut the puncher off.

He told the Stiles foreman, "Things are going well enough at camp, in spite of the trouble your friend Dab Pollard caused last night. But there just might be a storm blow in by evening, and in any event I need more men out there. I'm ordering every crewman now off duty to report before nightfall so they can spell the ones that are there and let them have their chance at a night in town."

Continuing to chew his food, Tate Corman heard him

out. "All right. You've spoke your piece; we hear you." He turned his back on the trail boss.

With no change of tone, Ben Murdock told the thick shoulders, "Pass the word to your friends. I don't want anyone claiming he never heard it. And I'll be looking for you all at the herd by eight o'clock, at the latest. I can't allow any exceptions."

He waited for an answer. Corman seemed to have dismissed him but he got a crooked grin from Gater. Murdock's jaw tightened. "Just remember what I said, Tate: no exceptions." He didn't expect an answer and he didn't wait for one.

As the screen door slammed behind them, Harry Griffith grumbled, "You can take my word—the sonofabitch means to defy you! Tate's got no intention of reporting, and if he don't, neither will any of his friends."

"I know," Murdock said.

"So what are you going to do?"

"Right now I figure to look in on Wally McKay."

"You know what I mean! I'm talking about Corman, and tonight."

"I guess we'll wait and see if anything happens. Meanwhile, I don't want *you* getting in any arguments with that crowd. But I'll appreciate it if you sort of move around, Harry, and see that the message gets an airing among the rest of our boys."

"Sure thing," Griffith answered. "I'll give the word to 'em: everybody in camp by eight. And they'll be there, don't worry. They know what's fair, if Tate Corman and his crowd don't. I just don't know what

157

you're going to do about *them*."

"My problem," Ben Murdock said, and let the matter drop.

CHAPTER XI

It looked to be an emergency meeting in the print shop of Tanner's *Gazette*. Besides Clark Tanner himself, two other members of the city council—Phil Steadman and Doc Riggs—were there. Over in a corner by the press, Tanner's compositor was busily sorting type, apparently working by touch. The tiny bits of lead whispered through his expert fingers as he focused his attention on the other men. The composing block at his elbow held a stack of freshly printed papers, the headline announcing Eden Grove's launching as a cattle market.

Ben Murdock had a copy in his pocket, but that had nothing to do with his presence in the shop. He had blundered in, not realizing a meeting was taking place, but no one seemed to notice him. On the verge of withdrawing, he caught sight of a man seated in Tanner's own chair behind the editor's desk, and something made him hold where he was, just inside the doorway.

There was a neatly brushed black bowler at the man's elbow, and a traveling bag on the floor beside his high-buttoned shoes indicated he had probably arrived on the morning train. He was short and rather stocky, with a head full of bushy dark hair, a narrow face, and a secretive look about him. Despite the sultry August weather he wore a suitcoat and a high collar, and he seemed to be paying the penalty for his vanity; he held a handkerchief with which he constantly dabbed sweat from his face and throat.

He seemed to be the reason for the meeting.

Mayor Steadman was speaking with what struck Murdock as a good deal of caution. "Suppose we start again at the top. So far all we know is what you've told Mr. Tanner. Your name is Giddings. . . ."

"Horace Giddings." The little man nodded briskly. "Attorney-at-law."

"Out of Wichita," Steadman went on. "We've already confirmed that we know the person you represent—Mrs. Rose Converse. Now exactly what is it you want this group to do for you?"

"Not for me," the lawyer corrected him. "For my client. And I'd like to say at the outset, Mrs. Converse hopes it will be possible to avoid any lengthy legal hassle."

"So do we, naturally. Which makes me wonder why she'd send a lawyer to talk for her. Why not come and talk to us herself?"

Giddings made a gesture with the hand that held the soggy handkerchief. "After all, gentlemen—a widow . . . alone in the world . . . she needs an experienced male to look out for her interests."

Clark Tanner said dryly, "I question that. She wasn't needing anybody when she showed up here last month, hunting for word of her husband. She'd traveled all alone, from Texas and across Missouri and half of Kansas, before the trail brought her to Eden Grove. And she was the one nailed the men who murdered

159

him, by recognizing her husband's ring on Nat Colby's finger. I'd have said Rose Converse was a woman who could look out for her own interests."

Watching unobserved, Ben Murdock guessed that the lawyer from Wichita was becoming flustered and more than a little angry, but if so he covered it up. "In a legal matter," he began, "that may call for court action. . . ."

John Riggs flung up a hand. "Let's not be in a hurry to talk about court action! This town has nothing but respect and sympathy for Mrs. Converse. Why would she think otherwise? If there's a problem, why can't she lay the thing out and let us see what it is?"

"That's what I'm here for." Giddings hurried on before he could be interrupted again. "Suppose we look at the facts of the case: Will Converse was a professional gambler, carrying his season's winnings when he started home for Texas sometime last fall. When he got this far he came on Nat Colby and Virgil Beason laying out their town. The two of them murdered him for his money belt and buried the body. Colby said later they took more than twenty thousand dollars off him, and used it to build and publicize Eden Grove.

"Beason was killed resisting arrest, and Colby's in jail at Hutchinson waiting trial for murder. Meanwhile, you men who call yourselves Eden Grove's city council have taken over as though the place belonged to you. It's my contention the largest part belongs to my client. Will Converse's widow owns a twenty-thousand-dollar claim to this town—a much bigger investment than anyone else."

Phil Steadman was on his feet. "Let's get a few things straight here!" he said angrily. "First, we only call ourselves the city council because a judge appointed us. As for 'taking over,' we claim nothing except our businesses and the building lots we paid for. Just now, it's true some of us have formed into a company, and we're dickering for a bank loan so as to buy out whatever interest Nat Colby still has in Eden Grove. He's bound to need every cent he can lay hands on, for fighting that murder charge. And after all, the town has to keep going somehow.

"These past weeks we've often wondered about the Converse woman, but nobody knew what had become of her. Once her husband's body was recovered and given a decent burial in the cemetery, she left without a word to anyone. It was as though she couldn't stand the sight of the place where he'd been murdered. I understand now, from you, that she's in Wichita. You go tell her we'll be glad to sit down whenever she wants, and talk about any claim she feels she has against Eden Grove. The court may rule, though, that she's going to have to recover it out of whatever we end up paying Nat Colby."

John Riggs added quickly, "You understand, there isn't a one of us who doesn't want to see justice done." Tanner confirmed the statement with a nod.

The lawyer frowned, obviously none too pleased. "If this is your last word," he said as he briskly got to his feet, "I'll pass it on to my client. But I can tell you now, I'll never accept any such ruling. You talk of justice. That's exactly what *I'm* asking—justice for a woman who suffered the agony of doubt all those months before she finally set out alone and found her husband had been murdered. There's no price can be set on an ordeal like that. All the same, I intend to get her every hard cent I can!"

"And lining your own pocket while you're at it?" Phil Steadman shook his head. "Save that oratory for the judge, Giddings! We have every sympathy for Rose Converse, but we won't roll over and play dead for any smart cowtown lawyer!"

By this time they were all on their feet, and the air of the print shop seemed to crackle with hostility. Across the room, Parley Newcome had left off work and was watching closely, with one hand full of forgotten type.

Horace Giddings found his voice. "Are you quite sure," he said stiffly, "that's the message you want me to take my client? Because in that case—" He snatched his bowler hat from the table.

Ben Murdock spoke up from the doorway where he had been a silent observer. "I wouldn't leave just yet," he said. As every eye turned to him he continued, "I may be butting in, but I think it'd be a good idea if you had a look at this fellow's credentials."

The three councilmen stared at him, clearly puzzled; the lawyer's face, after a first, startled reaction, was less readable. It was John Riggs who demanded, "Just what are you getting at, Murdock?"

"I'm only wondering if you actually know he represents Mrs. Converse. Unless he carries a letter from her or something, he could have come here on his own hook, meaning to work out a deal if he could and then try to cut himself in for a slice."

"What if I did?" the lawyer retorted, but there was a sudden undercurrent of anxiety in his voice. "Anyone has a right to offer himself as the go-between in a dispute."

Ben Murdock ignored him and told the council members, "It happens I've seen this man in action before, in other Kansas towns. I know the kind of jackleg reputation he carries. Let him mix into this, and I can wager you'll be sorry for it."

Horace Giddings' pale face was mottled with anger. Trembling, he cried, "Blast you, Murdock! I'll have you in court for libel!"

"Try it! I can find a couple of witnesses who'd more than welcome the chancc to tell you off in front of a judge."

Phil Steadman said, "What about it, Giddings? Can you prove that Rose Converse sent you? Any reason we shouldn't drop this until we can take it up directly with her?"

As Giddings looked around at the other faces it was clear he was fighting a losing battle. He tried to stammer something; then, furious, he jammed the bowler on his head and grabbed his traveling bag.

"The hell with all of you!" he cried hoarsely. And with no more ado he went storming out.

It had been a tempest, quickly ended. Clark Tanner limped over to the door and closed it. He turned and told the room, "Well, that's one meeting that didn't last long!"

Someone swore. Doc Riggs exclaimed, "Looks like

we owe you one, Murdock." Clark Tanner added quickly, "Here, have a seat. Let me pour you a cup of coffee."

The Texan shook his head. "Thanks all the same. I only mean to stay a minute."

"The things you told us just now—I take it you can vouch for them?"

"Maybe not the way you'd have to to print it in your paper," Murdock conceded. "But I know what I know. Otherwise I wouldn't have horned in on something that was none of my business."

"Don't apologize," said Phil Steadman. "I'd already made up my mind about that fellow before you spoke up. The way he tried to get tough with you, then backed down when you called his bluff . . ." He made a face, then added, "This isn't going to make trouble for *you*, I hope."

"Not a chance. I've got his number, and he knows it! I never meant to bust in on a meeting," the trail boss continued, dismissing the subject of Horace Giddings. "I was next door at the doc's office, looking in on my puncher to see how he's doing. Far as I could see he looked pretty good, but when he told me Riggs had stepped over here I thought maybe I could have a word and find out what the situation really is."

"I'm glad to say your friend is doing fine," the doctor told him. "Temperature's down and I figure the leg has a better than good chance of healing proper. All it takes is time, and keeping him quiet."

"He might bore himself to death. McKay ain't much of a hand at doing nothing. When I left, he'd started writing letters to everybody he ever knew back in Texas. Luckily he's got quite a slew of friends down there. And he's a slow writer."

A moment later the doctor left, claiming he had a call to make. Murdock started to follow him but held back, his hand on the door knob, as Clark Tanner said, "I understand you've already found a buyer for your herd, Murdock. Sounds to me you could hardly do quicker business than that, if it's true."

The Texan hesitated. "We found a buyer, only the deal fell through."

Mayor Steadman looked concerned as he came to join them at the door. "Fell through, you say? Chadwick didn't turn you down!"

"No, he gave us a good price, but we hit a snag on account of the peculiar way this drive was organized. So we'll just have to wait. When there's better news," he promised the newspaperman, "I'll see the *Gazette* has the story."

He turned back to the mayor. "Meanwhile, it just occurred to me: I know of quite a few outfits on the Chisholm right now, but like us not too many of them know for certain about your town, even if they've maybe seen the fliers. Don t you think you should be doing something about that?"

"How do you mean?"

"I mean, like sending some riders down into Indian Territory to meet those herds before they're committed to other markets. Let them know you're in business, with a sound drive trail all the way and a railroad at the end of it. If it'll help, you're welcome to use my name.

I'm known on the trail."

Phil Steadman had begun nodding as he listened. Tanner said, "You know, that strikes me as a damned good suggestion."

"We should have thought of it ourselves," the mayor agreed. "Thanks, Murdock. We're obliged to you."

"Don't mention it," the Texan said. A moment later, as he was going, he could hear the men earnestly discussing the Converse woman. Easy enough to guess that they'd find other matters less urgent, just now, than the troubling questions posed by the murdered gambler's widow.

In that morning's urgent summons to the herd ground, Ben Murdock had left most of his possessions at the hotel, including his shaving equipment. He had a heavy growth of whiskers, and even on the trail he tried to find time to take a razor to it at least once a day. Returning to his hotel room after the scene at the print shop, he got out his soap and worked up a lather with the tepid water from the commode pitcher. Scraping off the stubble, he had to be careful of the marks inflicted by Tate Corman's fists. Lazy village sounds came to him on the hot wind through the window, and once he heard something that could have been a rumble of far thunder in the clouds that were gathered just above the western horizon. Razor poised, Murdock listened for a repetition and wondered again if a storm was on its way.

He finished, cleaned his blade, and wiped the lather

from his cheeks. Dressed again and ready for the street, he got his hat, opened the door, and found Amy Grover on the other side of it with her hand poised to knock.

She drew back in surprise, startled despite the smile and greeting he gave her. "I was told you'd come in," she said, "and I brought your shirt." She held it toward him. "It's all washed and ironed."

And mended, he saw as he unfolded it to admire the neat workmanship. Any trace of damage had been removed, and the shirt looked as good as when he bought it new at Truitt's. Murdock didn't have to ask whose fingers wielded the needle and thread. With real admiration he said, "That's just fine, Amy! No one would guess anything had happened to it." He fetched a silver dollar from his pocket. "This cover what I owe you?"

"Oh, I couldn't take payment!"

"Nonsense! You don't expect me to let you do that for nothing. Here . . ."

But when he reached to take her hand and press the coin into her palm, she quickly backed from him, both hands thrust behind her. "Please!" she cried. "I *wanted* to." Just in time, he recognized the pride that would be hurt if he insisted on forcing payment on her.

"All right, Amy," he assured her, and returned the dollar to his jeans. "I'll just say it was mighty nice of you. And I thank you a lot!" She gave him a smile in acknowledgment and turned to go, but for some reason he found he didn't want her to leave yet. To hold her, he said the first thing that occurred to him: "How long have you worked at the hotel?"

The question surprised her but she answered it frankly. "Two months—a little more." She added ruefully, "It sometimes seems like forever."

"You're homesick, I guess."

Amy nodded. "I've never been away so long before in my life. Actually our farm's only about a dozen miles out from town, but it ain't all that easy for us to get back and forth. I've only seen my folks once since I moved to town."

Holding the shirt she'd repaired for him, Ben Murdock leaned on his forearm against the doorjamb. He considered the girl standing before him—the trim little figure, the head lifted high beneath its weight of dark hair. Genuinely curious about her, he asked, "Were you born around here?"

"Oh, no. In Iowa, actually. Except I don't remember it all that much. We came over into Kansas during the War, rented a farm outside of Severance for a spell— that's where my little sister was born. Then a couple years ago Pa decided to come farther west and take up government land for himself."

"I'd say homesteading sounds like a lonesome kind of life," Murdock observed, "for a girl growing up. Not many neighbors . . ."

She didn't deny it. "It's the truth. Here at the hotel, I see more people in a day than I'm likely to in a year at home. But . . . sometimes I feel a lot lonelier around all these people. . . ." She broke off with an embarrassed laugh. "Now isn't that a silly thing to say?"

"Not at all," Ben Murdock replied. "What about the future? Will you be going back? Or maybe there's some young fellow here in town you've got an eye on. . . ."

It had been meant innocently enough, but suddenly she was blushing, and tried to stammer something. He said quickly, "I'm sorry. I shouldn't have asked anything like that. Don't be angry."

But she was already edging away. "I . . . have to go now." She turned and hurried down the stairs, and left him standing there. He felt ready to kick himself for being too free with this timid homestead girl, spoiling their little talk. Now that she was gone, he regretted not being able to call her back.

At Harolday's, a few minutes later, he found the order for George ready for him in a brown burlap bag. Murdock signed the tab and carried the sack outside to lash it behind his saddle. While he was thus occupied a man pushed away from the narrow shadow cast by the storefront and came forward. It was Jay Gerringer. The marshal placed both hands on the tie rail and leaned his weight on them, observing the Texan at his work.

"Taking some stuff out to camp?" Gerringer commented, a remark that needed no answer. When Murdock didn't respond the marshal said, after a moment, "Care for a drink first?"

Murdock jerked a slip knot tight. "I guess not."

"Meaning that you won't drink with me," Gerringer interpreted, a shade tartly. "Suit yourself. I'd say you and I have been at crossed swords almost from the moment you arrived in this town."

That got him a long look from the other man. Murdock answered, "*You* said that, not me. Happens I just ain't thirsty."

"Hell!" In almost the first break Murdock had seen in his unruffled front of self-command, Gerringer gave the tie rail a hard slap with one palm as he wheeled angrily away. But at once he turned back, and he had himself under control again. "Look, friend Murdock," he said too quietly. "Why don't we have this out— while we can still do it with talk!"

"All right." Murdock left his horse and came to face the other man, with the tooth-marked pole between them. "I guess I don't like you much, Gerringer, but it ain't really personal so much as due to circumstances. After all, there's never much love lost in a situation like this one, between the town law and a crew just in off the trail and feeling its oats. Maybe it's a little worse here, since I take it you and I are both kind of in the same boat."

"Oh? How do you arrive at that?"

"Why, each of us has something he wants pretty bad, and it puts us at odds. I got a name as a drover I'm trying to build; you're in the second day of a new job, with somebody breathing down your neck and just waiting to see you make a bad mistake. So you go ahead and do your job," he finished. "But not at the expense of my people. Because I don't give a damn how hard Tom McDougall rides you—I won't have you passing it on to them!"

For a long moment the deepset eyes considered Murdock. "Then you, my friend," Gerringer said finally, "had better see that they keep the peace, and do it better

170

than they have up to now! If there are more disruptions like the one I heard about at Cotton's last night, or here on the street this morning, why, I'll be forced to hold you responsible!"

A sharp antagonism flashed between the two men as each took the other's measure. But there seemed nothing more to be said; Murdock simply acknowledged the warning with a scant nod. He turned his back, found the stirrup, and swung himself into the saddle. When he rode across the tracks, he thought he could feel the marshal's stare following him until unfinished buildings along Railroad Avenue's south side came between them.

CHAPTER XII

At the tail end of a long August afternoon, clouds that had lain against the western horizon freed themselves and spread halfway up the sky, hiding the sun and turning the river the color of pewter. An early dusk settled across the Arkansas flats. By ones and twos, men of the Pool crew who had been released to town the night before came drifting back, answering Murdock's summons that had been passed on to them by word of mouth. Some were hungover and grouchy, but most were good-natured enough about returning to their place at the herd. They had joshing exaggerations for the ones they were relieving, who were even now cleaning up and readying themselves for their own first venture to check out the fleshpots of Eden Grove.

Long before eight o'clock the trickle of returning riders had played out and ended. By that time almost all daylight had leaked away behind a solid shelf of clouds and night shadows were piling deep, stretching without a break between the wind-tossed flames of George's cookfire and the faint sheen of lamplight marking the town across the river.

Ben Murdock stood alone, looking thoughtfully in that direction and listening to the constant mutter of restless cattle. Lightning flickered intermittently, pearly against the clouds, but he caught no scent of rain. In the fitful glow of one prolonged run of lightning a trio of shadowy figures moved up to join him, their boots barely audible in the windwhipped grass. Vern Hoyt commented, "Well, Ben, is it going to hit us or ain't it?"

The pair with Hoyt were Ed Qualen and Harry Griffith. The latter observed, "The critters don't like it. Hear 'em?" They listened for a little, gauging from long practice the particular note of protest from animals bothered by the static electricity they were all conscious of. As for his companions, Murdock had a strong feeling something more than an approaching storm was eating at these men.

Hoyt said absently, "Well, we're set if it comes. . . ."

No one answered that and there was silence among them. Another flare eerily illuminated the empty grass that lay between them and the dark band of willows and scrub along the riverbank. Nothing moved out there, and Harry Griffith brought out what was in his mind: "No sign of Tate Corman—and it's past the deadline. I guess nobody's much surprised, though. He made it clear enough that him and his crowd would defy your orders."

When Murdock made no comment, Vern Hoyt shifted his boots in the grass and suggested, "Maybe it ain't really worth stirring up an issue over." Ed Qualen agreed quickly, saying, "Sure! Vern's right. We don't need 'em anyway. There's enough of us on the herd; we can handle anything that might come up. . . ."

Ben Murdock saw what they were after but shook his head. "No," he said firmly. "It ain't something I can just pass over. This is a challenge. Tate knows I got no choice but to take it up!"

"So you ride in looking for him," Hoyt muttered in a sour tone. "Then what happens? There's some kind of trouble. Next thing you know, that hardnosed town marshal mixes into it, and before you get through there's a real explosion. And all for what?"

Murdock patiently explained the obvious. "A trail boss who can't give an order and make it stick when he's challenged ain't going to last long. But more important than that, it's only a matter of fairness to the other members of the crew that I see to it every man draws his equal share of the work. I've got to go in."

"Alone?" Harry Griffith exclaimed hoarsely. "To face the lot of them? Not only the Stiles bunch; you can bet on it them Finches will be there to back 'em up. That makes eight altogether, primed and waiting!"

Murdock had counted the odds. "Not necessarily. This is between me and Tate Corman. I'm figuring the others will stay out of it."

"That may be how *you* figure," Vern Hoyt said bluntly. "We say you need us along to make sure. And don't tell us we ain't coming," he added, "because that'd just be *another* order you can't make stick!"

Murdock peered more closely at the three, realizing that this had been their real purpose in seeking him out. These were his most loyal crewmen, and the most dependable. Grateful, he finally nodded. "All right. Only, Sherm Watkins ain't back from town yet and that means somebody will have to stay with the herd to take charge in case that storm actually blows in or there's some other emergency. Ed, I'm going to ask you to do that; the other two can come with me. But I want it understood: Whatever happens with Tate Corman, you're to stay out of it unless I give you the sign. Is that plain?"

They had to be satisfied with the compromise. Ed Qualen looked disappointed at being left behind as the others went off to get their horses.

The fitful lightning made the horses nervous; so, too, did the wind that ruffled the grass about their hoofs and pushed against them. The wind covered other sounds. In the play of lightning, as they neared the river, they could see it toss the cottonwood crowns and the river-bank growth, where fireflies wove an intermittent pattern. The lighted windows of the town beyond the crossing grew larger and buildings began to take on blocky shapes.

Suddenly Harry Griffith saw something that made him exclaim, "Hey! What's that yonder?"

"Where?" Hoyt demanded. In the next brief flicker

of lightning he and Murdock both saw it. "It's a horse. Looks like it's hung up in the willows." All three now observed that the animal bore a saddle but no rider. With one accord they veered to angle in that direction. They were almost at the river; the muddy smell was strong where it made its way, gurgling and sucking, past a sand bar just beyond the willow screen.

They had not quite reached the horse when the animal managed to jerk free of the branches snagging its reins, and wheeled to get clear. Hoyt kicked his mount forward. When the other horse tried to swap ends he was able to trap the reins and pull it down, and they heard him exclaim, "I think it's Sherm Watkins' sorrel. Yeah—and his saddle. Hell, there's something wrong here!"

There was no sign of Watkins himself. Wasting no time with words, Murdock spurred past the others and began to work his way along the willow screen, listening and searching the shadows while his companions pressed after him and Vern Hoyt led the nervous sorrel. They nearly missed the dark shape lying face down under the willows. At once Murdock was out of the saddle, and Harry Griffith joined him. As the trail boss turned the limp body onto its back, Harry scraped a match against his boot and cupped it between his hands. The night wind that tossed the willow branches whipped the flame wildly and quickly extinguished it, but not before the light it cast on staring eyes, and on the bloody ruin of Sherm Watkins' shirtfront, told Murdock what he needed to know.

"Dead?" Vern Hoyt asked from the saddle, his voice

tight and hoarse. Harry Griffith, who had ridden half a dozen years for Watkins, let out a smothered oath.

"Probably within the hour," Murdock said. "He's not even starting to get cold yet. Must have been returning to camp when he got it—point blank. In all this wind and racket, sound of a shot wouldn't likely have traveled far."

"And he wasn't even wearing a gun," Griffith pointed out. "He never had a chance at all. . . ."

They grimly contemplated this thing that had been done. Wind rattled the dry willow scrub and thunder muttered somewhere far off. One of the horses started to move around uneasily.

Suddenly Harry exploded: "Damn that Dab Pollard!"

Ben Murdock looked at him. "Pollard? You think it was him?"

"Who else? Sherm kicked him out this morning, didn't he—warned him to stay clear of Texas. You heard the threats Dab was making when he left—and he's the kind that holds a grudge! I can picture him waiting around the whole day for a chance to pay off this one. Finally caught his man alone, rode right up and shot him at close range and let the sorrel carry him off and dump him."

"Dab Pollard!" The way Vern Hoyt said the name, it sounded almost like an obscenity. "I never gave the man another thought! I wouldn't of supposed he had the stomach for doin' murder. . . . But if he wanted to kill a man, this is probably just how he'd go about it."

"Likely we'll never know for certain," Murdock said. "It's useless looking for a trail before daylight, and even if that storm doesn't come in to wash it out it'll be cold by then. If Pollard waited around for his chance at him, he isn't likely waiting now."

"So what do we do?" Hoyt wanted to know as Murdock got slowly to his feet.

"I don't see what more we *can* do, aside from putting Sherm on his horse and taking him into town with us. I understand the man who owns the furniture store carries a line of coffins, and serves as undertaker. We'll leave the body with him, and then I guess it'll be up to me to send off a wire so Sherm's people can decide if they want him buried here or shipped home to Texas."

"I guess you're right." Hoyt cursed in weary frustration. "We may as well get at it."

Harry Griffith suggested suddenly, "We ain't forgetting something, maybe?"

"What?"

"Tate Corman . . ."

Murdock gave the puncher a startled look. It was true enough. Finding Sherm Watkins had for the moment knocked clean out of his head all recollection of the real purpose of their ride into town. Reminded, he frowned but he said sternly, "Everything in good time. Corman can wait. This has to come first. . . ."

Booker's Furniture Store, north of the tracks, was closed with only a dim light burning against the early dusk, but like most of the town's merchants Merv Booker lived behind his place of business and Murdock ordered Hoyt to go there, rouse the man and explain what was needed. "I want to get that wire sent right away. Afterwards I'll hunt up Doc Riggs and have him make out the death certificate."

"What about the marshal?" Vern Hoyt suggested.

"I don't want him involved, since it didn't happen in his town. I doubt anyone here so much as heard the shot. It ain't any of Gerringer's business."

"He may decide different when he learns about it."

"Let him."

Harry Griffith still had Tate Corman on his mind, and as Murdock started to pull aside toward the railroad depot the puncher said, "Might be a good idea was I to scout the street, find out just where Tate is at and what him and his friends are up to. Point is, they're still waiting to see if you got the nerve to take up their challenge. They don't know you got more important things on your mind right now. Their nerves are gonna be stretched pretty tight, and if they should have the first look you could be in trouble. Maybe it's best I tell them about Sherm and set them straight."

Murdock saw the wisdom of that. "All right," he agreed. "You just tell Corman not to be impatient. Once this matter's taken care of, I'll find the time for him!"

When he pulled away from the others, he took with him the image of Sherm Watkins' limp shape, face down on his saddle, his arms and legs rolling loosely to the slow movement of the sorrel as Vern Hoyt led it across the wide street at a walk. The night seemed to be changing. The wind was off, and the fretful lightning as well. An occasional rumbling of thunder suggested that the storm was swinging farther north, beyond the sand-

178

stone rim. If they were lucky, he thought, the weather might miss them after all.

Writing that telegram proved to be one of the toughest assignments Ben Murdock ever had handed to him, but there was no one else to do it and he was a man who always would rather have unpleasant chores behind him. Pencil stub in hand, he stared at the pad the telegrapher handed him and all he could see was the image of Sherm Watkins' sweetfaced widow. Just getting a wire was shock enough for anybody, and he couldn't think of any way to ease the blunt, stark message. He did the best he could, paid his fee, and left the window feeling shaken, and with an even greater anger building toward the man who had murdered Sherm Watkins.

He mounted and crossed the empty street, hoping to find John Riggs at his office so he could get the needed death certificate. He supposed there would have to be the formality of a hearing by the county coroner from Hutchinson, though it would serve little purpose. The usual verdict—"death at the hands of a party or parties unknown"—would do nothing to bring the killer to justice, whether it was Dab Pollard or some other person nobody knew about.

Riding past the corner entrance of the hotel he heard someone sing out his name. When he saw Jed Finch coming slack-jointed down the steps he grimaced and would rather have ridden on, pretending not to hear. Listening to whatever fresh complaint the man might have on his mind was something Murdock didn't think he needed just then. But an instant later he realized that

Watkins' death and Wilson Stiles's continued absence left Finch the only Pool owner now with the herd, and he resignedly pulled in.

He didn't dismount, and before the man could speak he gave his own news, mincing no words: "You'll be hearing this sooner or later. Sherm Watkins is dead."

For a long moment the eyes in the narrow face merely returned his stare, without expression. Murdock didn't know for certain whether the man was struck speechless or was not even surprised. But then, as though he belatedly realized that some kind of response was expected of him, Jed Finch shook his head and exclaimed in a leaden voice, "The hell you say!"

Murdock told it briefly: "He was shot, sometime earlier this evening. Near the river crossing. We just now found him and brought his body in."

"Anybody know who done it?"

"Not really." Ben Murdock lifted the reins. "I got to see if I can find the doc."

Finch shifted his gangling figure and lifted a bony hand. "The doc can wait," he said quickly. "Looks to me we got some serious talkin' to do."

"Maybe later."

"Later ain't good enough! It's you and me in charge of things now. There's matters that'll need threshing out, right off. Let's have us a drink and get them settled."

Murdock recognized that it was an order, not an invitation. He would have liked to refuse but something warned him, the way things were changing, he had better not. Relations between him and this man were already strained badly enough after that incident yesterday involving Amy Grover. He was going to have to deal with Jed Finch however little he enjoyed it.

He decided he really could use that drink. "All right," he said, stepping down to tie his horse. He ducked under the hitch pole and went up the steps where Finch waited. The glow of the porch lamp by the open door fell across their faces briefly as they passed through and into the lobby.

Murdock moved toward the bar entrance, but the other blocked him with an elbow thrust. "Not in there," he grunted, indicating the faint buzz of talk that came through the doorway. "Too damn public. I got a fresh bottle in my room."

Murdock nearly balked. A social chat in the privacy of Jed Finch's hotel room was about the last thing he wanted. He shrugged and said reluctantly, "It had better be quick."

"It will," the rancher promised. A tooth showed as he lifted his lip in a mirthless grin. "Believe me, I get no more pleasure than you do out of the thought of us settin' down together!" With no further comment he turned toward the lobby stairs and the two men climbed in silence to the second floor.

Besides Murdock's there was one other front room overlooking the street and Finch had signed for it. "Here we are," he said as he reached for the knob. Murdock noticed that he spoke much louder than he needed to—it could be a signal to someone within. The next moment the door swung open, and he realized that his half-formed suspicion was justified.

He would not have been too surprised to find Pike Finch sharing the room with his brother, and perhaps even with the hired man, Gater. And indeed Pike was there, sprawled on the bed with his booted and spurred feet crossed comfortably atop the bedspread, and Gater squatted on his heels in a corner with a brownpaper cigarette burning in his fingers. But there were three others besides. One of these Murdock had never seen before, but the man seated in the rocker by the window was Wilson Stiles. And there was the eye-filling bulk of Tate Corman, leaning against the wall beside the door and looking at Murdock with an expression that made it clear he had been ushered into a dangerous situation.

He halted at the entrance, his head lifting sharply. At once something sharp and painful ate into the flesh above his ribs, and as he jerked away from it he heard the voice of Jed Finch in his ear: "That's a knife, Murdock. Don't give us any trouble. Just walk in!"

CHAPTER XIII

Murdock didn't doubt it was a knife. Jed Finch was the kind of fighter who would carry one, and prefer to use it before he would a belt gun. He now knew Finch had been assigned to bring him up here. Now he had no choice but to let himself be shoved forward into the lamplight, encircled by watching faces. No one moved. Wilson Stiles said, "So you got him. Any trouble? Anyone notice?"

Before answering, Finch stepped back for a look into

182

the empty hallway. Closing the door, he said, "I reckon not. They wouldn't have paid any mind if they did. The town knows we're from the same outfit."

Stiles seemed satisfied with that. But he pointed out, "You were thinking you might have trouble persuading him."

"I had my little ol' persuader." Finch let the knife's blade reflect the lamplight briefly before it slid out of sight somewhere in his clothing. "Anyway he didn't object. He was too full of talk about Sherm Watkins being killed."

If Murdock expected a reaction to that piece of news, he was mistaken. No one said anything. Stiles's eyes narrowed, but it would have been hard to fathom the thought behind them. He told the newcomer, "Better have a seat, Murdock. And a drink."

He directed a jerk of his head and a snap of his fingers at Pike Finch, who reluctantly swung his legs off the bed to make room for Murdock to sit. There could be no doubt that the Finches were brothers. They had identical narrow features and prominent jaws and cheekbones. Though Pike was ten years younger, harsh Texas sunlight and a rough way of life had weathered them equally. Only the coarseness of the older brother's scalpful of hair indicated the difference in their ages.

Murdock had advanced as far as the foot of the bed but he preferred to remain standing, watching Stiles. He shook his head in refusal when the latter offered the whiskey bottle. Stiles, shrugging, put it back on the table and picked up his own glass.

Tate Corman must have been keeping silent only with great effort. Suddenly he burst out with, "What kept you, Murdock? Hell, this is way past the time you promised to come and boot my tail back to camp for me!"

"Sorry to keep you waiting," Murdock said dryly. "Is that what all of you were doing, cooped up here in this room?"

"As good a place to wait as any," Wilson Stiles told him. "You'd either have to show up or admit you'd lost your nerve. I was fairly sure you'd be along.

"Now you're here," he went on, "you may as well have that drink, because you're not taking any of my crew anywhere! There's something more important I want to take up with you."

"Yes! Let's get on with this!" The one who was a stranger to Murdock had been listening with a look of growing annoyance. He appeared to be the nervous sort, well and neatly dressed but ill at ease, fingers drumming the arm of his chair in growing impatience. He had wiry black hair and blue eyes that were seldom still. Of Wilson Stiles he demanded, "I want to find out once and for all: Have we a deal or haven't we?"

"Certainly we have a deal," Stiles assured him quickly. "Nothing's changed. The only question now concerns friend Murdock's part in it. This is Vince Crawford," he told the trail boss. "We met yesterday, in Ellsworth. Crawford is a buyer for a commission house in Chicago—never mind which one. He wants our beef. The exact details of his proposition don't matter too much either at the moment. But it's a very nice one,

184

and you've got a chance to be cut in on it."

"Me?" Murdock scowled at him, still in the dark. "You know I've got no say in selling this herd. I'm not an owner."

"You have friends in Texas who are. The wrong word in the wrong ears could spoil everything. That's why we have to be certain of you!"

Suddenly Ben Murdock's chest felt cramped; he drew a slow breath to ease it. "I reckon I'm beginning to understand. . . ."

"I'm sure you are," Stiles said, smiling coldly. "I never once doubted you were smart.

"It's simple enough: Crawford quotes a top price to his people in Chicago; I quote a bottom one to the folks in Texas. The difference is the pie we slice to suit ourselves. Of course, the Pool owners with the drive have to be cut in to make sure they keep quiet once they get home. Jed here was happy enough to take a share. But Sherm Watkins . . ."

Murdock was able to supply the rest himself. "Sherm wouldn't go along when he heard," the trail boss finished harshly. "Or sell out his friends at home who were relying on him to look out for their interests. And so you shot him! It wasn't Dab Pollard, or anyone else. It was *you,* Stiles!"

The man did not alter so much as an eyebrow. "With stakes as high as we're after, we can't bother with someone who won't keep his mouth shut." Deliberately Stiles finished his drink and set the glass down. As he poured himself another he added quietly: "How about *your* mouth, Murdock? Talking to Sherm, I gathered you were around when he made a deal with another buyer. What's it going to cost for you to forget all about that?"

"What kind of an answer do you expect from me?" Murdock retorted.

"I expect you to use your head." Wilson Stiles held the glass he had filled, turning it in his fingers so that the whiskey gleamed like an amber jewel in the lamp-glow. His eyes studied Murdock with mocking cynicism. "I got a theory about you," he said. "I've had your qualities flung at me till I've got a bellyful of them. The incorruptible Ben Murdock! I happen to think that *every* man has his price, if you only probe for it. That's what I mean to do with you!"

Ben Murdock said contemptuously, "How would you like to go to hell?"

Stiles's only reaction was a smug smile that barely turned the corners of his mouth. "Of course you'd have to say that," he told Murdock, his tone almost patronizing. "Now that it's said and we have the dramatics out of the way, let's get down to cases.

"I know you're an ambitious man, like all the rest of us; otherwise you wouldn't be in this tough business. Obviously you don't want to spend your life as a mere trail boss, working for other men's wages, when with a little capital you could hope to set up as a drover yourself, putting your own beef herds together and sending them off to market. You should be able to make a good start on five thousand dollars."

Ben Murdock had lifted a hand to the metal frame of the bed; his fingers tightened there until the knuckles stood out white beneath the stretched skin. Stiles must have taken that as a sign Murdock was weakening, and the thin smile became a smirk. "Seventy-five hundred, then. Am I getting closer?"

The smile turned mean as Murdock gritted, "You sonofabitch!"

Vince Crawford slapped a hand down sharply on the arm of his chair. "Getting closer, Stiles? You're not even in the same county. Hell, just look at his face! You'll never bribe this man—and you'll never stop him telling the world everything he knows."

"I'm not so sure," Stiles said.

"But I *am!* Now that you've talked so free, we're left only one choice and that is to get rid of him. Otherwise, our deal is off. I tell you, we can't afford the risk!"

It was an ultimatum. Watching Stiles, Murdock saw his eyes change subtly and then decision hardened the shape of his mouth. Ben Murdock knew his fate had been sealed.

He didn't wait. Jed Finch was standing so close he could feel the man's sour breath against his neck. Turning, one hand fumbling at his holster, he struck Finch across the chest with the other forearm and flung him aside. The closed door to the hall confronted him. As he started toward it, he was unable to remember if someone had turned the key in the lock after he and Finch entered. In any event it was the one slim chance he had.

He managed two long strides before his enemies' surprise wore off. There was an angry shout as Tate Corman catapulted from his lean against the wall. Mur-

187

dock whipped around. The gun he was trying to clear hung up in the holster, and an instant later he saw Corman's thick arm descending upon him.

He attempted to duck away but the blow landed, carrying all the weight of heavy bone and muscle. It took him precisely where the neck joined the shoulder. Murdock felt his knees start to buckle, a kind of paralysis seizing him. The gun popped out of a hand that could no longer hold on to it. He was going down, slowly but inexorably. His knees touched the floor and he fell face down full length upon the carpet. Then Tate Corman booted him in the side of the head.

White lights exploded before Murdock slid into a painful blackness, losing all awareness for a length of time that seemed like hours but was probably no more than seconds. Slowly his senses cleared enough to tell him he was lying on his face, the musty carpet odor sour in his nostrils and his skull throbbing. Arguing voices tumbled about him. It was Crawford, the cattle buyer, that he heard protesting, "But won't it raise a lot of questions if he just disappears like this and never shows up again?"

"No reason it should," Wilson Stiles retorted. "His job is finished. With Watkins dead, Finch and I represent the Pool. Who's to argue if we say we fired him and paid him off? What he did afterward is none of our business."

The arguing continued while Murdock listened and fought to clear his head. He made no attempt to move; he sensed that he still lacked the strength. He heard Tate Corman insisting, "Just make up your minds! And

188

somebody tell me how we're supposed to get him out of the hotel and out of town without nobody seeing. Especially if he's still alive!"

Jed Finch spoke up. "I sure as hell won't have him killed here in my room!"

"Does he have a horse?" Stiles wanted to know.

"Tied out front where he left it when I brought him up."

"Get it," Stiles ordered, suddenly all brusk efficiency. "Pike, you go fetch our animals. Take them around back to the alley and wait for us there. Whatever you do, act natural! Now get along. Both of you!"

Boots tramped past Murdock and the door slammed behind the Finches. After that Murdock's tentative grasp on consciousness must have slipped again, for the next thing he knew heavy hands laid hold of him and he found himself being dragged to his feet. Someone jammed his hat on his head. He thought it was Corman and Gater who had him, and he sagged between them as Wilson Stiles said, "Crawford, you'd best stay right where you are, out of sight. We don't want you seen taking any part in this."

"I haven't the slightest intention of it!" the cattle buyer told him.

Things commenced to happen fast. The door was flung wide. Murdock, hauled roughly out into the dimly lit hallway, tried to use his legs but they still lacked strength and let him down, a drag on the grip of the men who held him. He was roundly cursed and hauled up again. This time Gater and Corman each hooked one of his arms across their shoulders. With

Stiles in the lead, they hustled their prisoner along the corridor, legs dragging, between rows of closed and numbered doors and past the stairway to the lobby.

Ahead, a door at the hall's end stood open on darkness. When they dragged him through it, still groggy and suffering from a constant throbbing pain inside his skull where Corman had booted him, Murdock felt the cool air of the night against his face. It helped like nothing else to clear his head. Above him were stars where a sheet of clouds had hung a brief hour before. Looking down a steep flight of wooden steps he could see, in lamplight spilling from a window at the rear of the hotel, several horses being held in the alleyway and the faces of Jed Finch and his brother Pike, looking up.

The steps, between clapboarded wall and crude wooden railing, were too narrow for three big men. Tate Corman dropped back so Gater could go first, crabwise, with the prisoner between them. They struggled awkwardly to place their boots on the steps and maintain their balance.

Somewhere along the alley a man gave a sudden shout. The next moment a gun went off, the report a flat sound in the summer darkness.

The effect was startling. A horse squealed in terror while the men holding the animals ducked wildly, yelling out their alarm. Something seemed to have gone wrong, and now Ben Murdock, for a moment no longer the center of attention, thought he saw his opportunity. He brought up a boot toe sharply, catching Gater behind the knee, and with a cry Gater started to double forward as the leg gave way under him.

Murdock's arm was wrenched from Tate Corman's grasp. But Gater still had the prisoner by a wrist and Murdock felt himself going over, across the man's bent shoulder. He tried to grab for the handrail but missed. Helpless, he somersaulted over Gater's bent shape and his head and shoulders struck a lower step, hard. Then Gater's weight rolled down on him and they went tumbling down the flight of stairs in a tangle.

Murdock banged his head against a riser and nearly blacked out again. He was aware they had come to a halt. Head downward, on his back with Gater on top of him, he was able to look upward along the length of both their bodies and see Tate Corman looming above them at the top of the steps. A gun glinted in Corman's fist. The big man was beside himself, yelling obscenities furiously and flinging his arms about. Without warning he suddenly pointed his gun down the steps and fired. Murdock, horrified, felt Gater's convulsive jerk and heard his shout of pain as the bullet struck.

Corman had simply lost his head and triggered blindly, trying to kill Murdock without giving a thought to Jed Finch's cowhand. He looked ready to shoot again. Dimly aware of confusion in the alley—horses milling, men shouting—Murdock grappled with Gater, trying without much success to roll aside the inert weight that pinned him down. Suddenly he felt cold metal brush his fingers. It was the puncher's gun. He closed his hand on it and tried to drag it out of the holster, but Gater was lying on it and he lacked the leverage and strength to pull it free.

Tate Corman's weapon spoke a second time. Lead

struck the clapboard siding where Murdock's cheek was pressed against it, and the smear of muzzle flame blinded him.

Without warning another gun spoke, just behind him and close enough to shock his ears with its concussion. Still blinking through the afterimage following the blast of Corman's revolver, he saw the big man driven backward. Tate Corman struck the hotel's siding and caromed off it. He lost his footing, pivoted into the flimsy wooden handrail and took it out as he plunged to the alleyway below.

A horse lunged out of the way as he struck the ground, and then the only sound was of gunshot echoes fading. Someone laid hold of the moaning Gater and rolled him off Murdock. A moment later Murdock found himself looking up into the face of Jay Gerringer, and he heard the marshal saying, "Are you all right?"

Murdock tried to answer. Then strong hands were beneath his shoulders, helping to lift him, and he had to grit his teeth against the throb that had been put in his skull by Tate Corman's cowhide boot, and by his headlong tumble down the steps. In the alley Harry Griffith and another man he didn't think he knew had taken the two Finches prisoner and were getting no argument from them. Gater was moaning on the steps beside him, but there was no movement at all from Tate Corman, who lay like a bundle of old clothes where Gerringer's bullet had dumped him.

His head clearing a little, Murdock looked up at the doorway that stood open at the head of the steps, faint lamplight showing beyond. All at once he remembered something that shocked his dazed senses to life and made him fight his way to his feet. There was a gun in his hand, he discovered; he had kept it when Gater was rolled from on top of him. Ignoring Gerringer's exclamation, on uncertain legs he went blindly up the steps.

He stumbled over one of the risers and nearly fell, then reached the landing and rested a shoulder against the jamb of the open door. At the forward end of the hall Wilson Stiles was hurrying toward the lobby stairway. The bracket lamps burning on the wall appeared to have queer, bright haloes.

"Stiles!" Murdock called loudly.

The man turned, halting. Light from a wall lamp fell across his features as he came around to face the trail boss. All his arrogance was gone, replaced by a wary respect. He had a gun, and as Murdock started toward him he began to back cautiously away. The lobby stairs were very close now; watching his face, Murdock thought he might be judging his chances of reaching them.

From below, the voice of Vern Hoyt came up the stairway: "Ben! Ben Murdock! That you up there?"

Murdock drew a shaky breath, fighting the throbbing pulse in his skull. He managed an answer: "Vern? Stiles is here. Whatever happens, don't let him get past you. He's the one murdered Sherm Watkins!"

There was a startled oath, and boots hit the uncarpeted stairs. At the same moment Murdock heard someone behind him. Unable to take his eyes off Stiles, he could only hope it was the marshal, and from Stiles's expression he judged he was right. He saw the blond man waver, saw the swift fury break across his face. Trapped, and knowing it, Wilson Stiles let his hatred of Ben Murdock take hold of him. He swore bitterly in a way that telegraphed what was about to happen.

Murdock had never used a gun to kill, but taut nerves made his hand do its work now. The two shots were deafening, and came almost together. He never knew what became of Stiles's bullet; his own struck the cowman full in the chest. A gust of wind broke from the man's lips and his features convulsed in an agonized grimace. Then all the stiffness left him. He stumbled to a knee and then went face down, to lie without moving again.

Ben Murdock stood a moment over the man he had killed and tried to feel some emotion, but his thoughts were in muddled confusion. At the back of his mind something was nagging at him, and now it came clear as shouting men surrounded him there in the hallway where smoke still drifted. He stepped around the sprawled body and went directly to Jed Finch's room, brushing aside the hands and ignoring the excited voices. The door stood ajar; when he pushed it wide, the lamp that had been left burning on the table showed him the room was empty.

Murdock walked inside and paused by the table, where he laid down the smoking gun and looked around, still dazed. Vern Hoyt and Barney Osgood, from the desk in the lobby, followed him in. Hoyt sounded worried as he demanded, "Are you all right?"

Turning, Murdock asked hoarsely, "What became of

the man who was in this room?"

Hoyt, staring, could only shake his head and ask, "What man you talking about, Ben?" But Barney Osgood stammered, "Would you be meaning the one that come into the hotel earlier tonight, with—*him?*" He jerked his head toward the man lying dead in the hallway. "If that's who, then he left."

"Left?" Murdock echoed impatiently. "When?"

"Why, it was a few minutes ago—just about the time the shooting started out back. I saw him come down the steps to the lobby and out the door." Ben Murdock swore. The young fellow swallowed and exclaimed, "Was—was I supposed to stop him?"

Murdock made an impatient gesture. "No way you could have known . . . well, Crawford will have had time enough—he's quit of this town by now. And he ain't likely to be back!"

"Who was he?" Vern Hoyt demanded. "And what the hell's going on? You say it was *Stiles* that killed Sherm Watkins? Hell, we figured Dab Pollard—"

"We were wrong. He had nothing to do with it. For all we know, Pollard's miles away and still going." Murdock ran a hand shakily across his aching head. "Look, give me a minute, will you? I just killed a man—something I never did before. . . ."

"You look like something worse than that's happened to you!" Hoyt said. "You sure you ain't hurt someplace? I think you better sit down."

Murdock could have explained about the toe of Tate Corman's boot, and the further punishment he had taken in his spill down the outside stairway. Instead he said roughly, "I'm all right." He had caught sight of something lying just under the edge of the bed and he stared at it numbly. It was his own revolver, fallen or kicked under there when he was trying to get away from his captors. He didn't think he had strength enough just now to walk over and lean to pick it up.

"Something puzzles me," he mumbled, trying to focus his stare on Hoyt. "How did it happen you all showed up like this, just when I needed help? What was Gerringer and the rest of them doing out there in the alley?"

"Haven't you heard?" Phil Steadman said from the doorway. "It was the girl."

"Girl?"

"Amy," Steadman told him with a note of impatience. "Amy Grover, of course. She saw something made her think you were having trouble. . . ."

"What she saw," Vern Hoyt put in, "was Jed Finch marching you up the stairs to his room. According to her, you and Finch had already had some trouble, and so when the door shut and she heard loud talk in here, it scared her and sent her hunting help. I'd say you were lucky she found it in time."

"Amy?" Murdock repeated a trifle stupidly.

Then he saw her. She was in the doorway, behind Steadman. Her face was white, and to him there seemed to be two of her. His vision blurred, Ben Murdock started to take a step in her direction, and as he did the floorboards buckled and the musty carpet came up and hit him in the face.

CHAPTER XIV

For two days the big herd had been loading and moving east from the pens on the switch at Eden Grove, and there was enough of it left to fill one last train. Ben Murdock's share of the job, however, was done. With Sherm Watkins and Wilson Stiles both dead, and Jed Finch sitting in the jail at Hutchinson wildly confessing all he knew about the ill-fated kickback worked out by Stiles and Vince Crawford, there was no Pool owner left with the herd. So Murdock had decided to wire the Kansas City buyer, Chadwick, and accept his original offer. Money had changed hands; the crew was paid off. Some of the Pool cowboys had been instantly hired by Chadwick to help get the cattle into the pens and on their way to the slaughterhouse.

Half the remuda had been sold; the rest, together with the wagons, had already taken the long trail south with the riders who were returning to Texas. And on a bright August morning, with the bawling of steers sounding through the village as they were prodded up the ramps and into the cattle cars, Ben Murdock made a final visit to the doctor's office. He found Wally McKay sitting up in bed, the fever gone, his color good and only the slow knitting of the broken leg to hold him down. Murdock handed the puncher an envelope.

"Here's your pay, and your railroad ticket home to Texas," he said. "It will be a roundabout trip, but you've got lots of time. I don't want you traveling until the doc guarantees you're in shape."

McKay opened the envelope, looked at the green-backs it contained and then gave a low whistle as he unfolded the seemingly endless railroad ticket. He would be going by way of Kansas City and St. Louis to New Orleans, taking a stagecoach the rest of the distance. "Damn!" he exclaimed. "I ain't ever ridden the steam cars before. This is gonna spoil me for forking a saddle!"

"Then you'll be no use to anybody in Texas," Murdock warned him. "So you better not enjoy it too much. . . ."

John Riggs stood by, listening in amusement. He asked the trail boss, "How are things inside your skull, Murdock? No pain or nausea? No more double vision?" Murdock assured him that he felt fine now, and the doctor said, "That's good. Like I told you, you got yourself a concussion that night, but it looks as if it's cleared up."

Murdock told him, "I feel good enough that I'm going to be taking off shortly."

"Today?"

"In a few minutes. A bunch of the outfit's trailing back to Texas together. I've got a bank draft to deliver to the owners, and there's no further business holding me here." This was true. All bills had been settled with the merchants of Eden Grove. The sheriff and the coroner's jury at Hutchinson were satisfied as to the killing of Stiles and Corman, and both men had been buried in the cemetery atop a sandstone bluff north of town. Sherm Watkins' coffin had been sent to Texas in accordance with his widow's instructions.

Murdock told the doctor: "So I wanted to say goodbye, and thank you for everything."

"My privilege." They shook hands—strong hands, both of them, though one was tough and rope-burned, while the pale, spatulate fingers of the other man showed no sign of a callus. "Nothing more to say then, I guess," the doctor observed. "Except to wish you a good trip. And to hope I'll see you again."

"I hope that, too," Ben Murdock said.

His saddle roll was made up and lashed behind the cantle of the bay that waited at the hotel's hitching rail. Vern Hoyt, Harry Griffith, and Ed Qualen, his companions for the long ride home, had not yet made an appearance, and Ben Murdock felt the nagging of something personal left unfinished. Having pulled up the cinch and smoothed the saddle fender, he decided he must make one last effort to settle it. He turned to mount the hotel steps, and was surprised to find Jay Gerringer standing at the head of them, watching him.

The marshal could have just stepped outside, but he came unhurriedly down to join Murdock on the boardwalk. He nodded toward the waiting pony, the blanket roll and saddlebags that contained a rider's personal belongings. "I'd heard you were leaving us," he said.

"You seem to hear a lot," Murdock said dryly.

"My job."

There was a curious relationship between these two, each man wary, respectful, and yet with a definite wall between them despite the fact Jay Gerringer had probably saved the Texan's life with the bullet that killed Tate Corman.

Murdock said, "Considering the trouble it's caused, I don't suppose it will make you too unhappy to see the last of *this* outfit."

The other shrugged. "If not yours, it could have been the next one. But when the next one arrives, they'll find things a shade different." He turned his head and directed his brooding gaze across the street, beyond the tracks to the south side of Railroad Avenue.

Among other new buildings in the process of construction there, mingling the busy sounds of saw and hammer with the constant noise of bawling animals being shoved up the ramps from the loading pens, there was one squat and solid structure that stood a little apart from the rest. It was so nearly finished that a sign had already been hung. The newly painted letters, bearing elaborate serifs and curlicues, read: CITY MARSHAL'S OFFICE & JAIL. The construction looked solid, and the window that Murdock could see framed a mesh of strap iron.

He told the lawman, "That would certainly look as though you mean business. It also looks like something a Texas trailhand would as soon stay out of."

"Then," Gerringer said flatly, "if you bring another outfit here sometime, I suggest you try to see that your riders stay out of it. Because I'll never make an exception—not for you, Murdock, or anyone else. As long as I wear the star, my one concern in Eden Grove will be to keep this town in order. No matter who I might have to hurt!"

Ben Murdock met his look. His own face expressionless, he nodded. "I never once doubted it."

The lobby desk was deserted, and Murdock had already looked through all the likely places in the hotel—even poking his head into the kitchen—without finding any sign of the person he wanted. But the door to Phil Steadman's private office stood open and he walked toward it, a hand lifted to rap against the side of the jamb before he saw that Phil Steadman already had company. He would have withdrawn, but Steadman had caught sight of him in the doorway and the hotelman quickly rose from his desk, calling out, "Murdock! Come in, man. Come in! Here's someone I want you to meet."

He obeyed, somewhat puzzled because it was Sam Harolday he had seen standing near the window—a man he already knew and with whom he could have no imaginable business now that the Pool's tab at the store was paid. Then he noticed the woman who sat across from the desk. She was a stranger to Murdock, dressed for traveling. Conscious of his own sweat-stained hat, he quickly pulled it off as Steadman made introductions.

"Murdock, this is Mrs. Converse. I'm sure you'll remember that jackleg lawyer, Giddings, claiming her for a client the day you gave the council warning we should have nothing to do with him. . . ."

He had in fact forgotten. Now he remembered, and he looked with new interest at the woman whose gambler husband had been murdered and robbed by the founders of Eden Grove. She was a good-looking woman; dark-haired, probably some years older than himself, with a good figure still. He said something, and she told him seriously, "I'm indebted to you, Mr. Murdock. That man Giddings had been pestering me. I didn't like anything about him and I told him more than once I wasn't interested in doing business. But apparently he came here on his own, hoping to use threats and work up some sort of proposition, in my name, that he would be able to take advantage of. Believe me, I don't need anyone like him to talk for me!"

"I can believe that," he said, and meant it. She seemed a plainspoken woman, well able to handle her own concerns. He remembered what he had been told about this Rose Converse journeying alone from Texas in search of her missing husband, and turning up the evidence, unassisted, that had proved what became of him.

Steadman said, "One thing Giddings did do, without intending it, was give us a clue where she had gone after she left Eden Grove in such a hurry. She says she didn't want to make trouble for people who had nothing to do with her husband's death. But after that scene with Giddings I went straight to Wichita and sure enough I found her, and brought her back with me. We just got off the train.

"While I was at it I stopped in Hutchinson and talked to our lawyers, and to the banker. It looks pretty sure now that we'll get our loan, and our deal to buy the townsite. When we do, I'm going to insist that Mrs. Converse be counted in for a share. We're agreed that should compensate for her husband's money that was stolen and put into developing Eden Grove."

"Will the others go along?"

"I think I can guarantee it. Meanwhile, here's Sam Harolday who has a proposition to buy the store he's been managing. He'll pay for it out of his profits, and I intend seeing to it Rose Converse gets those payments. . . . I have to say, by tipping us off to that Giddings fellow you did us all a very real service."

Ben Murdock said, "I'm glad to think so." He glanced at Harolday. He didn't much like the store-keeper, who struck him as an angry and discontented man, unhappy to be the manager of someone else's business. But if he could get ownership, it might at least create a better atmosphere in the Harolday house-hold. Murdock hoped so; he had felt sorry for Lucy Harolday.

He asked Steadman, "You got a couple of minutes? I'm leaving, and there's something I want to ask you."

"Leaving?" Murdock explained about his friends, due at any moment to join him and start the long ride to Texas. The hotelman exclaimed, "Are you sure John thinks you're up to it? I know the day I left for Wichita, he was worried about that concussion you took." The trail boss assured him the doctor had declared him fit. Steadman excused himself to the man and woman in his office, and the two of them stepped out into the lobby.

Steadman was full of enthusiasm this morning. He said, "I've been told another trail herd moved onto the flats last evening."

Ben Murdock confirmed it. "I was talking to the trail

boss; he says he knows of two more coming in behind him. Looks like the runners you sent down the trail are getting results."

"And we don't forget it was your suggestion. So what can I do for you, friend Murdock? Name it!"

A little embarrassed, the Texan said, "I just wanted to ask you about Amy Grover. I'd like to say goodbye, but I haven't seen her around the hotel this morning."

"This is Tuesday, her day off. She may have gone to see her family. They have a homestead a few miles from Eden Grove."

"That's what she said." There was real disappointment in Murdock's voice. "So I guess I won't be able to see her after all. Would you be good enough to tell her goodbye for me?"

"Of course." And then, as the sound of arriving horses broke upon the stillness of the street outside: "That could be your friends. Have a good trip, Murdock."

"I expect to. Thanks. . . ."

They were all there—Vern Hoyt and Harry Griffith and Ed Qualen, mounted and ready. Something of their eagerness for the trail was communicated to their animals; the horses stirred restlessly, raising the powder-dry dust. Hoyt had a packhorse anchored to his saddle by a tow-rope, to carry grub and supplies for the long trek back down the Chisholm. When Murdock appeared all three riders sent up raucous greetings, cursing him genially and upbraiding him for losing time and making them wait. Ben Murdock grinned and retorted with the same friendly banter, then swung down the steps and ducked beneath the tie pole.

He had his hand on the reins, ready to jerk them free and lift into the saddle, when something at the shadowed end of the hotel veranda caught his attention. There were more groans and protests from his friends as they saw him change his mind and head again for the steps. "You'll have to wait a minute longer," he told them over his shoulder.

The girl came out of the shadows to meet him. Murdock pulled off his hat. "Amy!" he exclaimed. "You should have said something. I almost didn't notice you there."

"I just thought I'd like to see you off. . . ."

"We'll soon be on our way." He indicated the trio of horsemen in the street. "But I've been hoping for a chance at least to say goodbye. After all, if it hadn't been for you giving the alarm that night, I likely wouldn't even be standing here. I'll always be grateful."

She shook her head quickly. "I wouldn't want you thinking you owe me anything!"

One of the riders raised an impatient shout and the others joined in. Harry Griffith yelled, "Kiss her, and let's ride!" and got Ben Murdock's angry look.

He turned back to the girl. She stood gravely before him. The roof shadows against the contrasting white light of the morning obscured her features but he could tell that her expression was wholly serious. "Look," Ben Murdock said hurriedly, "I really got to go. But next year I aim to be back, whether with this outfit again or some other."

"Or a herd of your own?" she suggested.

He smiled. "That's rushing things a little, maybe. But one way or another, I'll be around. And when I do, I'd like to look you up—if that's all right."

Her smile answered his. "I hope you will," she said.

"It's a promise." In that moment he knew that he could indeed have kissed her. Her face was lifted toward him, the expression of her eyes sweetly willing beneath the dark sweep of hair across her forehead. But that would have unleashed a chorus of good-natured teasing from his friends in the street, and he didn't want that to be part of the memory he took with him. And so, regretfully, he satisfied himself with a single brief touch of his hand upon her shoulder. "Until then," he said.

He left her there and returned to his horse. With a single fluid movement he caught the reins, put his toe to the stirrup and rose into the saddle. A last look and a lift of the hand, and then Ben Murdock kicked his horse to join the others. They went with a whoop and a rush. A shod hoof struck a single clanging stroke on a rail of the Santa Fe's tracks, and after that they were across Railroad Avenue and the buildings of Eden Grove fell behind them. The broad and beaten trail to Texas beckoned them south.

Center Point Publishing
600 Brooks Road ● PO Box 1
Thorndike ME 04986-0001 USA

(207) 568-3717

US & Canada:
1 800 929-9108